Fruitful Affair

C. L. Conolly

FRUITFUL AFFAIR

KILLER WORDS PUBLISHING
Copyright © 2021 by C. L. Conolly
Cover photo by EPiC
Author photo by Julie Moore Photography

C. L. Conolly
www.clconolly.com
clconolly@gmail.com
New Ulm, Texas

ISBN-13: 978-0-9886876-4-6

Printed in the United States of America

10 9 8 7 6 5 4 3 2 1

Fruitful Affair

Thank you so much to all my beta readers and editors for all the help with perfecting my story lines and making sure I only put out the best stories for all my readers.

Also written by C. L. Conolly

<u>Lone Titles</u>
Friendly Misfortunes

<u>Affair Series</u>
Forbidden Affair
Family Affair
Fundamental Affair

One

Jasper and I were finally preparing for our honeymoon. As I relaxed on the bed, hoping that my re-mutilated stump would heal, my phone rang. Picking it up off the nightstand, I noticed the call was coming from an unknown number, but answered the phone anyway.

"Hello?" I said, as soon as the call connected.

"Mackenzie, it's Amber. I need your help," a female voice said, on the other end of my cell phone.

"Amber, you are not supposed to contact me," I told her.

"I need your help! Please, I don't know what to do," Amber pleaded with me.

"I'll let Agent Leigh know you called," I told her, pulling the phone away from my ear to hang up.

"No Mackenzie, please!" I heard Amber yell, just before touching the red button and hanging up the phone.

"I thought Amber was supposed to disappear and never contact you again," Jasper said, as I tossed my cell phone on the bed.

"That's what Faith told her. I don't need this stress right now," I told him, sliding to the edge of the bed allowing my one leg to hang off and rubbing my forehead with the heels of my hands.

"Call Faith and I will finish repacking for our honeymoon."

Jasper was swapping out certain clothing items that had been originally packed due to the fact that the season had changed. Pants were swapped with shorts and long sleeves were put away and tank tops were packed. I had decided that I wanted to be comfortable on our honeymoon, so I was going to wear shorts and ignore the fact that my legs were different.

Faith Leigh was an FBI agent who was the police officer who found me when my mother abandoned me when I was six years old. I had recently found out that my biological father was Detective Rage. The police detective who assisted in the investigation of 'The Butcher' case. Malachi Townsin was a sick son of a bitch who abducted and mutilated women for his own sick amusement. It turned out that he was my biological brother and he had amputated my left leg and raped me. I was left for dead in a plastic storage box at the back door of the hospital. Months later, when he killed my friend, I shot and killed him.

After opening *The Ansley Kirkland Center for Recovery,* in memory of that friend, Amber Harwell came to stay at the center, lying about who she was and what happened to her. She turned out to be my biological sister and was helping Detective Rage, who's real name was Brett Carter, to finish my murder. Amber changed her mind at the last minute and killed our father. Faith Leigh showed her mercy and told her to leave town and to never contact me again.

"Faith, I just received a phone call from Amber. She said she needs my help," I told her, as soon as she answered the phone.

"What phone number did she call you from?" she asked.

I gave her the number from my recent call list and she told me she would take care of it. I hung up the phone and continued to focus on my impending honeymoon. The week went on, business as usual, as I waited for my final doctor's appointment so I could wear my prosthetic leg again.

When Amber had manipulated me into joining her on a road trip to a dilapidated cabin, Detective Rage, or technically Brett Carter, was there and had abducted Rebecca Simms, who was identified as my biological mother.

My mother had abandoned me when I was six years old at a hotel. I spent the rest of my childhood moving around from one foster home to another. I thought I would never see her again until recently when she decided to return to my life.

By the time Amber and I had arrived at the cabin, Brett Carter had already amputated Rebecca's leg and she was bleeding out. Amber tied me to a chair and Brett decided to flay my stump.

I was out of commission until the doctor gave me the go ahead to wear my prosthetic again. Until then I was confined to a wheel chair. Jasper and I had to put our honeymoon on hold, again, due to the fact that he knew I wouldn't be able to enjoy myself until I could walk.

I had a doctor's appointment five days after I was released from the hospital, as well as ten days after. My doctor required me to attend physical therapy in order to become reacquainted with my separate appendage.

"You're doing pretty good. It's like you're a natural," Katrina, my physical therapist, told me.

"Well, I've had to put on my leg like an accessory for about a year now. I hope I'm a natural at walking with it," I told her, as I spun like a ballerina on my good leg.

"Well, look at you. You sure do look comfortable walking around on that thing. I think it's time that you and Jasper go on your honeymoon. Go, relax and forget about all your troubles," the doctor told me, as he came into the therapy room.

"Then we better get back to the center and let everyone know we are leaving," I told Jasper, who was sitting in a chair along the back wall in the room.

"Let's get going," Jasper said, taking my hand and leading me out to the car.

TWO

Jasper and I called for a center meeting with my sisters, Charlotte and Jillian, along with Gabrielle, the one who saved Ansley, the center's namesake.

"Okay everyone, Jasper and I are finally leaving for our honeymoon. I need each one of you to work together and hold down the fort," I explained to Charlotte, Jillian and Gabrielle.

Charlotte and Jillian were my foster sisters. I went to live with them after more than a dozen failed foster homes. We had been together for more than half my life and they were the only family I could depend on, other than Jasper.

Gabrielle was the woman who had saved Ansley Kirkland. Malachi Townsin, 'The Butcher' had amputated her left leg, assumed she had died and disposed of her body in a plastic storage box on Gabrielle's property.

After the news had reported my story, Ansley found me and we had become friends. When the two of us returned to the home I was abducted from, Malachi broke in and slit Ansley's throat, just before I shot him in the face with a shotgun. I named the recovery center in her memory for her son, Matthew, who was the product of Malachi's rape.

"No problem Kenzie. We've got this taken care of. You go, relax and enjoy yourself for the next two weeks. You deserve it," Jillian said.

"I really need this vacation. I just have to make sure that the three of you can work together without any drama. All I can hope for is some resemblance of normalcy. I won't be able to relax if I think there will be animosity here at home," I said.

"You mean me, don't you?" Gabrielle scoffed.

"Yes Gabrielle, I mean you. Not only toward Charlotte and Jillian, but also toward the guests here at the center," I told her, matter-of-factly.

"You know Mackenzie, you are the only one here I have a problem with. After what you did to Ansley, I hold animosity toward only you. I get along just fine with Jillian and Charlotte," Gabrielle said, smirking at me.

"Regardless of what you think of me Gabrielle, I would like to be reassured that you are not going to push aside the guests concerns, no matter how stupid you think they are," I said, pursing my lips and raising my eyebrows.

"I will take care of the guests and make sure they come directly to me with any concerns they may have. That way, I will be the only one to deal with them, so you won't have to worry," Jillian told me.

"Okay Jillian, I trust you to cover it from here. Charlotte, please assist Jillian with anything she may need. Also, Gabrielle, you are to report to Charlotte while we are gone. Jasper and I will be back in two weeks. In that time, no one is expected to be admitted, or leave, so it should be pretty easy for y'all. If you need me for any reason, please do not hesitate to call me."

"I'm pretty sure we can handle this," Charlotte reassured me.

"I'm talking about the children. If any of the foster children need our guidance, please call me," I requested.

"I assure you Mackenzie, I will take care of them just as you do," Jillian said.

"Good, Jillian will take care of the children and no one needs to disturb us on our honeymoon," Jasper said, glaring at the others.

"It's okay if they call me for the kids," I told him.

"You belong to me for the next two weeks. They don't exist and your focus should be on me," Jasper told me, as he grabbed my upper arm.

"Okay, I get it. Go pack the car so we can leave," I told him, kissing him on his cheek.

Jasper let go of my arm and headed out of the center. As soon as the front door closed, I turned toward my sisters and Gabrielle.

"He's being a little aggressive, isn't he?" Charlotte asked.

"More possessive than aggressive," Gabrielle agreed.

"He's just trying to get some alone time with me. We haven't had any since we got married. Shit keeps hitting the fan," I commented.

"How about you call us if you need help," Charlotte said.

"He's my husband and he loves me. He won't hurt me," I attempted to reassure them.

After loading our luggage into the car, Jasper re-entered the center as I hugged my sisters. Jillian was always more compassionate than Charlotte, but Charlotte still held more compassion than Gabrielle.

"You ready to go, Mac?" Jasper asked, placing his hand on the small of my back.

"Yes, absolutely yes," I said.

"Enjoy and make sure to relax. We will take care of everything here, so don't worry," Charlotte said, as we headed out the door.

"I'm so glad we are finally able to do this. We both need to relax and clear our minds. No more worrying about a psycho killer," I told Jasper, with a sigh of relief.

"Well, I can say that trying to figure out who the killer is, was pretty exciting," Jasper said.

"Oh yeah, it was a blast. You only say that, because the killer wasn't after you. Just because your biological family isn't a group of murderous psychopaths, doesn't mean a crazy, stalking, killer, stranger won't someday come after you. You're a good looking man and women can be crazy. Maybe one day you show a nice courtesy to a woman who thinks you are flirting and becomes obsessed with you. Then she decides she's mad that you're married and kills you out of jealousy."

"Wow, that was pretty specific, but if she is obsessed with me and is upset I'm married, wouldn't she just eliminate the competition so she could have me all to herself?" Jasper said, smirking.

"Nice, so I'm having to dodge another killer? In this scenario, you are the target because she has decided if she can't have you, then no one can. Plus, I'm tired of having to fight off the killer. It's your turn," I explained, laughing.

"This is an extremely morbid conversation."

"It absolutely is, but this is how our life is now. We get to wonder about everyone around us and if there might have been something we said, or did, to possibly trigger someone's murderous rage."

"Alright, Mac. Let's hope the rest of our lives is just as exciting as the beginning has been."

"Oh, you want excitement? How about you pull over and we get our honeymoon started early?" I said, placing my hand on his knee and slowly moving it up his thigh.

"Well, seems like someone has finally relaxed a little and has decided to relieve some stress," Jasper said, shifting in the driver's seat, leaning toward me in the passenger seat.

"There is only one way I know how to relieve stress, but I'm going to need your help," I said, leaning over from my seat and kissing him on his neck.

"Can you wait until we get to the resort? It might be a little weird and awkward if we stop at a motel for an hour just to relieve a little stress. Plus, we have two hours to catch our flight," Jasper said, quaking in his seat.

"Fine," I said, sitting back in my seat, crossing my arms over my chest and smirking.

"We are ten minutes from the airport," Jasper informed me.

"Oh, is that what you want? You want to sneak off to the bathroom before our flight?" I asked, rubbing his thigh again.

"That's not what I meant," Jasper said, smiling.

"You are such a tease, but I love you. I hope you plan to take advantage of our alone time," I told him, sliding my hand a little further up his thigh.

"Okay, here we are," Jasper said, pulling into the parking lot at the airport.

Three

After a six and a half hour flight, we had finally landed in Hawaii. We held hands as we strolled through the airport on the way out to the shuttle.

Jasper had made reservations for us at a five star, all inclusive resort and spa. Everything we needed was located in or around the resort, so we could walk.

When we disembarked the shuttle, we were greeted and each given a lei as well as a cocktail that tasted like pineapple. Jasper wandered over to the front desk in order to check in, as I admired the aesthetics of the lobby. There was a sweet, crisp scent that wafted throughout, with soft, soothing music enveloping around me.

I took in a deep breath and closed my eyes. It felt as though a huge weight had just lifted off my shoulders and floated away. As I opened my eyes, Jasper stepped up behind me and wrapped his arms around my waist.

"I have the key to our happy little getaway. You want to go with me?" Jasper asked, softly pressing his lips against the back of my neck.

I turned around and cupped his face in my hands. "Oh, we are going to the room, or all these people here in the lobby are going to get a show," I said, pressing my pelvis against his.

We walked toward our assigned room with our arms wrapped around each other. At that moment, I felt as though I finally had a normal life.

As Jasper opened the door to the room, it looked like a small one bedroom apartment. There was a tiny kitchen with a refrigerator, coffee maker, microwave and a sink. The living room furniture was set-up facing a large sliding patio door, overlooking the ocean and beach area.

As I slowly wandered through the room, I felt all the stress and tension that had built up over the past couple of years just slough off and every muscle in my body relaxed. The bedroom was only large enough for a king sized bed with a night stand on each side. There was a dresser against the wall approximately two feet from the foot of the bed. The attached bathroom had a stand up stall shower and a large jet tub along with double sinks. The entire square footage of the suite was probably four hundred with the largest square footage in the living room. I figured it was because anyone staying in a place that beautiful, wouldn't spend much time in the bedroom.

Jasper took our luggage into the bedroom and placed it on the bed, as I opened the large sliding door and stepped out onto the patio. There was a small rectangular table with a two seater bench on one side, which looked out to the ocean. There was a beautiful floral arrangement placed in the center of the table.

I sat down on one side of the bench at the table on the patio and looked out at the beautiful view. I closed my eyes and took a deep breath, relaxing. As I opened my eyes, Jasper stepped up behind me, placed his hands on my shoulders and kissed me on the top of my head.

"How beautiful is this place?" I asked Jasper.

"It's amazing," he said, slowly moving his hands down my body and over my breasts.

"What's going on here?" I asked, with a sensual tone.

"How about we go in and test out the bed," Jasper said, moving around to the front of me and presenting his hand.

I placed my hand in his and he pulled me up into his arms. Our lips met and our tongues tangled with each other. Jasper swept me up into his arms and carried me to the bedroom. He gently placed me down on the bed, slowly removed my prosthetic leg, then he laid down on the bed next to me. He was passionate, gentle and loving. The whole time my mind was focused on him and the way our bodies intertwined with one another. We were completely in sync with each other's movements as his hands gently caressed my body as he thrusted.

We both climaxed at the same time and Jasper slowly lowered himself onto the bed as he pulled out, then snuggled into me. The two of us were still panting heavily for a few moments after.

"You want to go for a walk along the beach?" I asked, as soon as I was breathing normally.

"We can walk along the part of the beach within the boarders of the resort. We are at an adults only resort, so you can focus on yourself and us along with being in the moment. I feel like your mind isn't fully with me when we are alone in our room together," Jasper said, kissing me on the cheek and getting out of the bed to assist me with my prosthetic limb.

"You know me so well," I said, kissing him after he put me together and assisted me into a standing position.

We got dressed and headed out to the beach. I was so glad he had packed shorts for me. The weather was beautiful, but it was warm enough where we were both wearing shorts, so we could walk along the shore with the water coming up and splashing our feet.

We meandered down the beach until we came to an outdoor bar. Jasper asked if I would like to get a drink and it felt like we were on our first date again.

Jasper walked up to the bar and asked for the most exotic drink they made. The bartender nodded, grabbed a couple of pint glasses, mixed several different liquids together in a metal shaker, then poured the mixture into the glasses. He topped the drinks off with a pineapple and cherry garnish and handed the drinks to Jasper. After payment was made, Jasper turned and handed one of the drinks to me and we wandered off to find a place on the beach to sit down. My stump was beginning to throb and I wanted to remove my prosthetic.

We found a couple of chairs to relax in and sat down to enjoy the view. I placed my drink down in the sand and unstrapped my left leg from the stump. Jasper took the prosthetic and placed it down at his feet. I retrieved my drink and sat back to relax.

Jasper and I watched the ocean roll up onto the sand, then retreat back into itself. The drink was sweet with an alcohol after burn I felt all the way down my chest. I sipped it slowly due to the fact that I wasn't much of a drinker and I hadn't had any alcohol since I had opened the recovery center. As a matter of fact, since most of the guests were on medication that couldn't be mixed with alcohol, it wasn't allowed in the center.

After a few moments of quiet reflection, a couple stumbled over in front of where we were sitting. The man had short, brown hair and was wearing swimming trunks with a plain white muscle shirt. The woman had her blonde hair pulled up into a pony tail and was wearing a bikini with a silk wrap around her waist.

"Whoa, Sara. Check it out. She can take her leg off," the man said.

"Dustin, you can't say things like that out loud in public. I'm sorry ma'am. When he drinks, he's like a toddler with no filter. He just says the first thing that pops into his head," the woman apologized.

"No problem. I can understand how startling this must look. Sometimes I wake up and forget that it's missing and fall out of bed. I look down and yell, 'oh my goodness. Someone stole my leg while I was sleeping'. Then I just stare at my stump until I remember," I said, smirking.

Jasper snorted as he stifled his laughter.

"Oh man, for real?" Dustin asked, dumbfounded.

Jasper and I both leaned into each other and giggled.

"She's kidding," Jasper told him, between breaths.

"Damn, that's fucked up. I just about lost my buzz feeling like shit because I can't control my mouth. I'm sorry, okay," Dustin said, sounding offended.

"Considering I'm the one missing my leg, I feel entitled to make jokes about it. Maybe I should have overreacted like you did. How about y'all sit down and I'll tell you the story of what happened. I'm not offended by anything that anyone says. If my joke upset you that much, I hope we don't run into each other again while we're here," I said, calmly sipping my cocktail.

"Naw, I was kidding. So what happened?" Dustin said, sitting down on the sand in front of us.

"Have y'all heard about 'The Butcher'?" I asked, as Sara joined Dustin on the sand.

"Wasn't that some sick fuck serial killer?" Dustin asked.

"Yes, he was a sick fuck serial killer. He took me, tortured me and amputated my leg. Now, I live with people staring at me and wondering what happened. I would prefer for people to ask questions, rather than make snide comments. Now then, I'm Mackenzie and this is my husband, Jasper. We are finally taking our honeymoon and we are here for two weeks. How about y'all?" I told them.

"Well, I don't think our story can top that, but I'll give it a shot. I'm Sara and this is my foster brother Dustin. We met at a foster home when I was twelve and he was fourteen. We both aged out of the system and moved in together. Recently we decided since we are the best relationship we have ever had, we are going to have a baby together. So we are technically on a baby moon. It's like a vacation right before the baby comes. As soon as we get home, we are going to the fertility clinic and having our baby put in me," Sara explained.

"We were both foster kids as well and met at the same age as y'all. We recently found each other again after being separated. Although, we were basically in love when we lived in the foster home together," Jasper explained.

"That is so cute. We are just like regular siblings other than the fact that we are having a baby together," Sara began, as she rubbed her belly. "We have never had sex like you two obviously have because you are married to each other, but we went to a fertility clinic and had our stuff scientifically fertilized and I am going to carry a baby that is a part of each of us. We get along so well together, that we decided that we would make great parents together," she continued and lightly punched Dustin on his bicep. "Everything we have is separate so we don't fight about finances because we pay our own bills. We don't fight about sex because we don't have sex with each other."

"We are very happy together and have never seen each other as siblings," I said, sipping my drink.

The four of us shared horror stories along with good times from being in the foster care system until the sun went down. At that point, Jasper and I had enough alcohol in our system, we were definitely inebriated.

"How about we go eat at the resort restaurant," Jasper suggested.

"That would be nice. I could definitely go for food," I said, as I attempted to put my extra appendage on my stump.

"Dude, I think it's on backwards," Dustin laughed, pointing out that the foot was positioned wrong.

"I have definitely had too much to drink," I said, laughing along with the others.

"Let me help you," Jasper offered, as I leaned back and laughed hysterically.

I hadn't laughed that hard ever in my entire life and it felt great to get it out. Dustin and Sara were laughing with me and Jasper was smiling as he strapped on my leg.

Jasper helped me up and we headed toward the resort restaurant. We ate and had several more drinks. Sara and Dustin seemed to be great people, but Dustin kept asking about 'The Butcher'.

"So he was someone you knew?" Dustin inquired.

"I didn't really know him, he was just the creepy guy from the diner we frequented," I told him, sighing heavily.

Jasper noticed I was becoming irritated and he decided to end the evening. "Okay, I think it's time for bed. We are getting tired."

We said good bye to our new friends and went back to the room. We had barely got undressed before we passed out on the bed to sleep off the alcohol.

Four

When I woke up the next morning, Jasper was standing outside on the patio. I could hear him talking to someone, seeing he was on his phone.

Before I could join him, the poison I had ingested the night before decided to exit my body. I placed one hand over my mouth and thankful that I had passed out with my prosthetic still attached, I rushed to the bathroom to vomit.

Once my stomach was empty, I backed away from the toilet and sat down on the floor across from it, leaning against the wall. As I wiped my mouth with my shirt, Jasper entered the bathroom and squatted down next to me.

"Had a little too much to drink last night?" he asked, brushing the back of his fingers along my cheek.

"Maybe just a little," I said, chuckling. "Who were you on the phone with?"

"Oh, it was nobody," Jasper said, ignoring my question. "So what are the chances of you wanting to eat?"

"Outlook not so good," I said, reciting the magic eight ball.

"Well, you might want to eat later. How about we just hang out here in the room for the day and maybe we can order room service when you are ready to eat," Jasper suggested.

"That sounds amazing. I don't know if I could take another day with Dustin if we happen to run into him and Sara," I said, rubbing my forehead.

"Okay, let's get you back into bed," Jasper said, assisting me into a standing position.

We spent the entire day two of our honeymoon in bed. We not only made love, we also enjoyed each others company.

The third day of our honeymoon, we woke up early to go out to the resort restaurant for breakfast before we went to the spa. While we were eating, Sara and Dustin came over to introduce another couple they had met the day before. The man looked similar to Dustin other than the fact that he had blonde hair and the woman had her chocolate brown hair pulled up into a pony tail, similar to Sara. All four of them were dressed to go swimming.

"Hey guys. This is Mackenzie and Jasper," Sara began, introducing us to the new couple. "This is Hallie and Camden. We met them yesterday and we told them all about you. They really wanted to meet you."

"Really, well then. Hello Hallie and Camden. How are y'all doing this morning?" I asked, standing and shaking their hands.

"Can we see it?" Camden blurted.

"See what?" I asked, knowing full well what he wanted.

"Your amputation," Hallie whispered, taking a seat at the table with us.

"That is completely inappropriate. I'm going to respectfully ask all of you to please leave us to finish our breakfast. If you refuse, I will contact the security and have you removed. It has been nice meeting you Hallie and Camden, as well as seeing you two again Sara and Dustin," Jasper politely told them, standing and leaning over the table, palms flat on the surface, making direct eye contact with each one of them.

"Well, they got to see it the other day," Camden said, disappointed.

"I'm not a sideshow attraction. What gives you the right to come over to me and ask to see the mutilation a psycho cursed me to live with for the rest of my life?" I yelled, loud enough for the entire restaurant to look over in our direction to see what was going on.

A restaurant staff member came over and stood next to the table. "Is everything okay over here?"

Jasper sat back down and took a deep breath before responding. "I'm sorry, we didn't mean to disturb everyone."

"These people came over to ask me to remove my prosthetic leg, so they could see my stump," I told him, being snarky.

"You four are going to have to leave. Please don't bother the other patrons," the restaurant employee requested.

"Okay, I'm sorry. Maybe we will see you out on the beach later," Sara said, as she turned to walk away.

When the others remained at the table, just glaring at me, Jasper stood up and placed his arms around the shoulders of the guys, leading them to the exit.

I watched as Jasper walked out of my line of sight, it looked like he was having a friendly conversation with Dustin and Camden as Hallie lagged behind them. It seemed a little strange that Sara and Dustin had walked in and headed straight toward our table. It was as if they knew we were there. The fact that they brought in another couple to harass me, was completely inappropriate and I was glad that Jasper recognized that. What I couldn't get over was several red flags that had recently come out about Jasper.

He was portrayed as being aggressive and possessive before we left the center. He was secretly talking to someone on the phone and refused to tell me who it was and now he seemed to be having a friendly conversation with a couple of guys who were harassing me after he went off on them.

I wasn't sure what to think about his behavior, but I was positive he only had good intentions. He was a laid back guy, so I attributed his friendly conversation as his way to get his point across.

"I have scheduled a full spa day for us. They are also aware of your extra appendage and have made arrangements to accommodate you. We are first scheduled for a couples massage. Let's get to that and we can relax on the beach later when we are done. The entire spa treatment I have scheduled for us will take about four hours to complete. If you're not relaxed by the end of the treatment, then they didn't do it right," Jasper told me, after he had returned to the table.

"I hope it does help me relax. I feel like the only reason I really snapped like that was because I am so tense," I explained.

Once we had finished breakfast, Jasper and I headed to the resort spa. Through the front doors, the lights were dim and there was soft relaxing music playing through the speakers in the ceiling. A woman sat behind a short counter and greeted us in almost a whisper.

"Hello and welcome. What is the name on your reservation?" the woman asked.

"I think I put it under Tully," Jasper told her.

"I've got you right here. We have a double room set up for you and your masseurs are ready for you. If you give me a few moments, I will call them up here and they will escort you back to the room," the woman told us.

After a few moments, two women appeared in the hallway and greeted us. We were escorted into a massage room with two massage tables set up. The women waited outside for us to prepare for the treatment. Jasper and I undressed and laid down under the sheets provided. We only waited a few moments before there was a soft knock on the door and the two masseurs came in. One masseur came over and whispered in my ear.

"We know about your prosthetic. Would you mind removing it? It might be easier to massage the stump without the extra piece," the masseur said.

"Of course. Sometimes I forget it's an accessory," I told her, sitting up in order to unstrap my prosthetic.

The masseur took my left leg and set it aside as I returned into position so she could rub my back. Immediately, I felt all the muscles in my body relax. She started at my shoulders, making her way down to my lower back. She not only massaged my arms, but she also rubbed my hands. Once she was done with my upper body, she made her way down to my thighs and down my right calf. When she began rubbing my right foot, it was almost as if all the frustration and tension had just left my body.

"Okay, ma'am. You can roll over," the masseur told me, as she lifted the sheet in order to cover me.

Once I was settled on my back, she replaced the sheet over me. I closed my eyes, relaxed onto the table and the masseur gently began to rub my face.

She placed a warm, wet cloth over my face and moistened the skin. She massaged a gel cleanser onto my face, then wiped it off with the same warm cloth. Then she massaged an exfoliating scrub onto my face and wiped it off with a new warm cloth. After that, she placed a gel sheet mask on my face and massaged over the mask, rubbing the gel substance into my skin not only on my face, but around my neck and shoulders.

When she pealed the sheet mask off, she then massaged the remaining gel substance into my skin before whispering she was done. I laid there for a couple of moments, enjoying the feeling of relaxation before slowly sitting up and draping an oversized robe over my body that the masseur had left on a chair next to the table so I could reach it. Jasper walked over and picked me up in order to placed me into a wheelchair to take me to the next spa treatment.

"Do we just leave our stuff here?" I asked Jasper, as he wheeled me out.

"I have a key to the room to lock it up to keep our items safe. We will be coming back here for another quick massage before we are done," Jasper said, as he turned to lock the door.

He wheeled me out to a sauna room and assisted me with wrapping a towel up under my arms to cover my exposed breasts under the robe. We were the only two in the sauna at first, so Jasper carried me over to the bench seat and placed me into a seated position. He folded the wheelchair and placed it against the wall just inside the door and draped our robes over it. Jasper sat down next to me and we both leaned back and relaxed to enjoy the purging of our pores.

It was only a few moments before four more people entered the sauna. I opened my eyes and looked up to see Sara, Dustin, Hallie and Camden. I exhaled loudly feeling the tension return to my body. Jasper looked up and just nodded at them to acknowledge their existence.

"Oh man, isn't this a coincidence? Check it out," Camden said, pointing at my stump peeking out from under the bottom of my towel.

"Can you please not speak. We are trying to relax," Jasper requested, saving me the angry outburst.

Camden shrugged and joined the others on the bench seat, as Jasper and I leaned back to relax again. The four others whispered to each other, as they discussed my stump.

"Do you think she would let me touch it?" Camden asked.

"I don't think she would allow that, but at least you got to see it now," Dustin told him.

"You do realize that this is something tragic that happened to her and not something that she did for attention," Sara scolded.

"Her story was public. That means she should be willing to show people," Camden said.

"You can be such an asshole sometimes," Hallie said, to Camden.

"For crying out loud! SHUT THE FUCK UP!" I shouted.

It became quiet and the four of them finally quit whispering. After we had been in the sauna for an hour, a spa representative came in.

"Mr. and Mrs. Tully, your rose bath is ready," she said.

Jasper stood up and walked over to retrieve our robes and the wheelchair. He wrapped the robe around me and carried me over and placed me into the wheelchair. The spa representative held the door open as Jasper wheeled me out and we followed her into a room with a large rectangular pool like tub in the center of the room. The tub was full of steaming water with rose petals floating on the surface.

The spa representative left the room and Jasper assisted me with removing my robe and towel and he placed me down into the water. I relaxed into the tub as Jasper entered on the other side and relaxed across from me. The tub was long enough for the two of us to sit on opposite ends, facing each other, stretched out and our feet wouldn't touch. The soft scent of roses filled the air. Within a couple of moments, a couple of women entered the room without speaking. One woman sat next to my right side and began massaging my hand. The other woman tended to Jasper. The ladies focused on our hands, arms and shoulders. Neither one spoke, they just ensured we were relaxed.

Once the ladies were done, they left the room and Jasper once again assisted me. Using my arms, I pulled myself up and out of the rose bath, sitting up on the edge. He wrapped the robe around my shoulders and I slipped my arms into the sleeves.

Jasper brought the wheel chair over near me and lifted me up. He helped me into a seated position and wheeled me back to the massage room we started in. Once he had unlocked the door, he pushed the wheelchair up next to the massage table and scooped me up into his arms.

Before placing me up on the table, Jasper softly pressed his lips to mine. I disrobed, laid face down and draped the sheet over my lower half. The same two masseurs came in within just a few moments.

The masseur stepped up next to me and pulled the sheet up over my back, up to my shoulders. She first rubbed her hands over my back as if she were smoothing the sheet, before placing warm stones lined down my spine and across my shoulders. At that point, I was so relaxed, I began to doze off.

Just before I had entered the rem stage, I was awoken by the masseur lifting the stones off my back. Once she was done, she tapped me on the shoulder.

"I'm all done," she whispered in my ear. "Take as much time as you need before you get up. Your husband should be done soon."

"Thank you," I whispered.

The masseur left the room, as I reached my hand around and grabbed the sheet to cover myself. I rolled over to face the side of the room Jasper was on and allowed my right leg to hang over the side of the massage table before sitting up. I rubbed my eyes, trying to fully wake up.

As I pulled my hands away from my face, I peered over and realized that Jasper was not lying on the massage table next to me. I looked around the room thinking that maybe he was still in the room. Once I noticed he had disappeared, I tried to lower myself down on my right foot, so I could get my prosthetic and dress myself in order to find him.

I held onto the massage table and I did what I could for myself. When I reached for my appendage, the door to the room opened and Jasper walked in. I turned to face him with tears streaming down my face.

"Mackenzie, why are you crying?" Jasper asked, without acknowledging the fact that I was standing with one leg.

"Where did you go?" I practically whispered, as I tried to stop crying.

"I had to go to the bathroom. You were asleep and I thought I would be back before you were done," he told me, as he walked over to assist me back to sitting on the massage table.

"I don't know what is going on with you, but I want you to go back to being the Jasper you use to be."

"I'm still the same I have always been. What are you talking about?"

"Nothing, never mind. Forget it. I'm probably looking for something that isn't there."

"Okay well, let me help you."

Jasper helped me strap on my left leg, then turned to grab my clothes. He faced me with my clothes draped over his arm and handed me one piece of clothing at a time.

Five

Once we had stepped out of the room, the masseurs were waiting for us with mini metal water bottles filled with berry water. We took the bottles from the ladies and headed to the exit. As we meandered back to our room, holding hands, I decided to just focus on being in the moment.

As we made it back into the room, I picked up my cell phone off the bedside table to see if Charlotte or Jillian had called from the center. They seemed a little concerned about Jasper's behavior before we left. After the few unusual behaviors I had noticed, I was wondering if they would call to check on me.

There was a notification on the screen, which showed I had a missed call and a voicemail, but I didn't recognized the number. I unlocked the phone, pressed the widget for the phonebook app and touched the voicemail icon. I went ahead and pressed play to listen to the message. In order for me to be able to change my clothes as I listened to the message, I pressed the speaker and placed the phone back onto the bedside table.

"Mackenzie, it's Amber. I'm being followed by someone who says they know you. Please help me. She is threatening me. Wait! No!" was all that was said on the message.

"What is her problem? Doesn't she understand she is not supposed to contact you?" Jasper asked.

"I'm just going to forward the message to Faith and move on. I am feeling so good after the spa, that I don't give a shit what she wants," I told him. "I am out of fucks to give about Amber."

I decided to change into relaxed clothing to ease my anxiety of possibly being harassed about my prosthetic again. Luckily, Jasper had packed a pair of baggy sweat pants and a camisole for me.

"How about we go take a walk along the beach," Jasper asked, as he emerged from the bathroom, once we had both changed our clothing.

"That would be amazing. I just hope we don't come into contact with Dustin, Camden, Sara and Hallie. I mean, the ladies aren't too bad, but the guys are assholes," I told him.

"I understand. They were a little overbearing at the spa."

"A little? They were completely out of line. What kind of people ask someone to show them their amputated limb?"

"Let's just relax and try not to think about them. Let's just enjoy the rest of our honeymoon," Jasper said, lightly kissing me on my cheek.

"You're right. We did just enjoy the most relaxing time we have had in a long time. We should enjoy it while we can," I agreed.

As we strolled down the beach, we allowed the water to roll up on the shore over our bare feet. We were trying to just concentrated on our breathing and relaxation. It was amazing enjoying our time together alone, without any interruptions.

"How about something to eat?" Jasper asked, after about an hour.

"That would be nice," I told him, as we walked up the beach toward the resort restaurant.

Even though it was mid afternoon, we stopped for lunch. I was actually feeling a state of euphoria from just being able to focus on myself. It was just the two of us and my phone didn't ring the entire time we were sitting there. I was so glad we were able to appreciate each other without anyone interrupting us.

For the rest of our honeymoon we didn't see Dustin, Camden, Sara, or Hallie again. To make things better, I didn't receive another phone call from Amber either. Of course, I wondered if she was safe, but did everything I could to push those thoughts out of my mind.

Jasper took me to the spa twice more, in order to receive different treatments. He had disappeared a few more times and had been on his phone secretly talking to someone, he wouldn't tell me who it was. I decided he was probably trying to surprise me with something, so I let go of any suspicion I had and just enjoyed myself.

By the time our honeymoon was over, I was so relaxed and happy, I had forgotten about my past and was really looking forward to my future.

Six

I was practically skipping as Jasper and I stepped through the front doors of the center. Charlotte and Jillian were sitting behind the reception desk talking. They looked up simultaneously as we approached.

"Welcome back. How was your honeymoon?" Charlotte asked, as she stepped around to the front of the desk and hugged me.

"It was wonderful. The spa was absolutely relaxing and the view was serine. We had the best time. How are the children?" I asked.

Jasper and I decided that a section of the center was to be allocated for foster children who were having a hard time with life. We took them in, in order for them to receive the direction they needed to become functioning members of society and to keep them off the street.

There were several juvenile offenders Jasper and I took straight out of a juvenile detention center and turned them into upscale citizens. We allowed all of the children to stay at the center until they were ready to support themselves. The age range of the children in the care of the center was between twelve and eighteen. The few foster children we had that were over the age of twenty, had already moved out, but every-so-often a couple of them would show up just to visit.

"The children really missed you," Jillian told me.

"I want to set up a special dinner for them. I want to make this weekend nothing but fun for our foster children. Jasper and I would like to sit down with each one and see how their lives are going. Where are they right now?" I asked.

"Lavender took everyone upstairs about an hour ago. Kensington was the only one having an issue without you here, but Lavender took care of him and he seemed to calm down after a couple of days," Charlotte informed.

"Why didn't you call and let me talk to him? My poor sweet King. I'm going to go check on him, just to make sure he knows we are back," I said, heading toward the staircase.

"Honey, they should be coming down for dinner soon. You can talk to him then. You know if you go up there now, he is going to cling to you for the rest of the night and I'm sure you want to do a few things before dinner," Jasper told me, touching my shoulder.

"You're right. I'm going to set up a fun party for the children. This is going to be great. I'm going to make a plan right now and create a questionnaire to give each one of them to find out what kind of activities they would prefer," I said, heading toward my office.

"It's nice to see you in a good mood," Charlotte said.

I turned and smiled before stepping into my office and closing the door. The first thing I did was call Agent Faith Leigh. I was curious about Amber and why she was contacting me.

"Hey Faith, it's Mackenzie," I said, as soon as she answered the phone.

"Mackenzie, how was your honeymoon?" Faith asked.

"It was amazing. I really needed the time away," I told her.

"Were you able to relax and forget about everything that has happened?" she inquired.

"Jasper had spa sessions set up for us almost every day and the massages were amazing."

"That's awesome. I'm so glad you were able to relax. So, are you calling to inquire about Amber?"

"Yes, what is going on? Did you get the message I forwarded to you?"

"I did. I was able to meet with her and find out what was going on. Do you remember Angela?"

"Are you talking about the girl from the first foster home I lived in?" I asked.

"That's her. She is now Angela Spitzer. The home she and Gwen were sent to after y'all left Betty Warren's house, was a cult family. Social services weren't aware of the cult mentality of the family when the girls were placed there. At the age of eighteen, Angela was married to a thirty five year old man who already had three wives. When Gwen turned eighteen, she became that same man's fifth wife. Angela's first child was born within the first year of being married, as was Gwen's child.

"Their husband, Gary Spitzer, demanded each of his wives to have a child every year until God decides it is time to stop. The women and children must follow the man of the house. The men are to follow the high priest who follows God's law. Amber happened to come into contact with Angela by accident. Angela approached her in a diner. Amber said that Angela knew who she was and sat down at the table with her. Amber mentioned a teenage boy who was with Angela. She said he was very intimidating," Faith explained.

"What does Angela want with Amber?" I wondered.

"That's where it gets crazy. According to Amber, Angela told her that you have a damaged soul and you must repent of your sins. She says you are being haunted by a demon and that is why you have had the recent tragedies in your life. She requested Amber help her get through to you, or Angela's family will come after Amber. Amber is terrified. The first phone call you received was right after the initial meeting. The group is apparently following her and watching Amber's every move. She is terrified that if you don't contact Angela, the group is going to kill her."

"How am I supposed to contact Angela? Did Amber tell you how I was to contact Angela?"

"She said they would find you."

"What does that mean?"

"Amber told me that before she contacted you the first time, Angela had just approached her out in public, but after I had contacted her directly, she stated that Angela and Gwen, along with each of their oldest children, had cornered her at her home. They tortured her into telling them where you were. Someone had informed them that you had left town on your honeymoon and they wanted to confront you and your husband."

"They wanted to confront Jasper and me for what reason?"

"Angela seems to think that if you become pregnant before you repent, you will give birth to a demon spawn who will create Hell on earth."

"Is Amber okay? Did they injure her? Was she hospitalized?"

"She did spend one night in the hospital, but I have placed Amber in protective custody for now," Faith told me.

"They should be arrested for what they did to her," I said.

"Unfortunately, we are unable to gain access to the religious compound and they have their own police along with their own border patrol. We are limited to what we can do with the compound having their own law enforcement. If the citizens living at the compound leave the boundaries, then we can question them to get information within probable cause to get a search warrant. Unfortunately, the high priest has managed to brain wash everyone at the compound and the children that were born there, are all loyal to their leader. No one is willing to talk," Faith explained.

"Am I in danger?"

"I don't think so, but we will keep watch on the center just to be sure."

"Sounds good. I'll make sure our private security is aware of the police presence," I told her, before I hung up the phone and booted up my computer.

I took a deep breath before preparing the questionnaire for the foster kids. I wanted them to feel included in the decision of food and game choices for the party. They always had someone around for emotional support, but I felt as if the kids were missing the personal family connection.

Also, with the possibility of danger from Angela, I was planning to confine myself to the center in order to ensure my safety and the safety of my children. I was hoping that Angela would eventually lose interest in whatever she wants with me and would move on to some other crazy cult sacrifice. I didn't want to have to worry about her and her henchmen possibly injuring me, or a guest of the center. The center was my halidom and I wasn't going to allow anyone to take that away from me.

As I printed the questionnaire, I set up a surprise secret movie night, that would only include the foster kids. I wanted to have Jasper set up the projector in our room, so we could invite them in to watch a fun movie.

I pulled the papers off the printer and as I straight-ened them on my desk, someone knocked on my office door.

Seven

I swiveled my chair toward the door after minimizing the document on my computer screen.

"Yes?" I said, without getting up from my seat.

The door opened slowly. Rebecca Simms poked her head in. I quietly sighed with agitation due to the fact that I had been trying to avoid coming into contact with her during her stay at the center.

"Mackenzie, can I talk to you?" Rebecca asked, as she entered the office on crutches.

I wanted all of my guests to feel welcome, even if I didn't care for them personally. I scratched the back of my neck and waved her in. She was trying to be a part of my life, but I never wanted a relationship with her. When I was a kid, I held on to hope that the police would find her and she would save me from the shitty foster homes I kept getting placed in.

Once I was placed in the house with Charlotte and Jillian, I had come to terms with the fact that my mother was never coming back. After everything I had been through, I never wanted to see her again. One thing I wasn't opposed to was faking being nice.

"You are walking pretty good on those things. When did you swap out the wheel chair?" I asked cordially, as she closed the door behind her.

"Last week while you were gone. Did you have a good time on your honeymoon?" she asked, as she crutched over and sat down in a chair across from me on the other side of my desk.

I didn't exactly want to engage in small talk with her, but her demeanor since the incident had changed. When I had first met her, she seemed self absorbed and attention seeking. I loathed the actual existence of her. After she had been admitted into the center, she became timid, shy and reserved. I no longer had a strong hatred for Rebecca, but I generally steered clear of seeing her regularly.

"It was nice and relaxing. What can I do for you?" I asked, deciding I was done with the niceties of small talk.

"Gabrielle's brother is going to fit me for my permanent prosthetic tomorrow and I was wondering if you would be willing to go with me," she requested.

I wasn't sure what to say at first, seeing as I didn't really want to have a personal relationship with her. I just stared at her for a few seconds trying to come up with an excuse not to spend time with her.

"I will be throwing a party for my foster children this weekend. I'm arranging games and food, but I will see what I can do," I told her.

"Okay then, thank you for your time," she said.

She slowly positioned her crutches in order to assist herself into a standing position. Looking over at me, most likely thinking that I would change my mind as I watched her struggle, she slid the crutches under her arms and slowly made her way out of my office.

Rebecca left me feeling uncomfortable and I thought my response to her was slightly petty, so I picked up the receiver of the phone on my desk and dialed the extension to the reception area.

"Could the two of you please come into my office," I asked.

"Sure," Jillian agreed and they were standing in the doorway within a minute.

"What can we do for you?" Charlotte asked, as they sat down in the chairs across from me on the other side of my desk.

"Rebecca was just in here asking me to go with her to get her permanent prosthetic. It was really awkward," I told them.

"What did you tell her?" Charlotte asked, curling her upper lip.

"I told her I was planning the party for the foster kids and had a lot of work to do to get it organized on time, but I would see what I could do. I didn't want to commit to spending time with her," I said.

"Are you ever going to give her a chance?" Jillian inquired.

"Hell no. I don't want to give that bitch any of my time, or attention. She didn't want to spend time with me when I was a kid and I don't want to spend time with her now," I responded.

"She wants to correct her relationship with you," Jillian said.

"There is *no* relationship. She is just a guest here at the center. Thank you for that, Charlotte. In other words, I'm going to be professional and cordial to her, the same as I am to the other guests. I don't want to hang out with her," I told them.

"Rebecca approached us when you were on your honeymoon and asked if you might be willing to talk to her. We told her, she needed to approach you and ask if you would be willing to talk. We didn't know she was going to ask you to go with her to get her prosthetic fitted," Charlotte informed me.

"Let's move on. I need you to take these questionnaires to the foster children and inform them about the party. Let them know I would like them back by dinner time so I can begin the planning process and order what needs to be delivered. Also, make sure they know that it is suppose to be a surprise for the other kids in the center, so they don't say anything to anyone else. I don't need the mom squad questioning me about why I'm excluding the guests. Everyone living in the center is invited to the party, I just want my kids to be included in the planning stage," I told them.

I picked up the stack that was resting on my desk. Giving half the stack to Charlotte and half to Jillian, I leaned back into my chair and sighed heavily.

"I'm sorry Mackenzie. I didn't realize that you were still trying to avoid Rebecca. I promise the next time I come into contact with her, I will not engage in a conversation about you," Jillian said, tears welling up in her eyes.

"It's not your fault. What Rebecca did was inappropriate. Next time she asks about me, please just tell her that she is here for personal healing and not for personal relationships. Jillian, I love you, but please stop being so sensitive. I'm not mad at you," I said.

"Why are you crying? It's not like she yelled at us. Come on Jilly. Let's get these to the kids so they have time to think about their responses. Go to the bathroom, wash your face and compose yourself," Charlotte said.

Jillian and Charlotte left the office, closing the door behind them. I pulled up the internet on my desk top and looked at a moonwalk renting website.

I reserved a bouncy house along with an inflatable water slide. The foster children had come to the center feeling as though they didn't have a voice. Each one of them had spent time in foster homes where they were forced to do things they didn't want to do and were not able to voice their opinions. Jasper and I wanted to make sure these kids felt as though their opinion counts.

We had noticed some of the parents who reside in the center with their children don't agree with our parenting stance. I had heard at least five different mothers complain that Jasper and I give our foster children too much reign within the center. These five mothers were lead by one woman, Jenny, to which I wished we could have kicked out. Unfortunately, she had three children and none of the staff believed in forcing children to become homeless.

This woman would gather her group of hens and complain about the foster children. Sometimes Jasper, Charlotte, Jillian, or I would have to come between these women and the foster children. The group would berate and bully the children until most of them were crying. We have all had one on one therapy sessions with each woman instructing them to leave my foster children alone.

After the third time we had an issue, four of the women have since stopped bullying my children, but they stand behind their leader and allow her to berate them. Any time I bring up her moving out and living somewhere else, she cries and plays to my sympathy for her children.

Before I ordered any food, or decided on any other activities, I had to wait for the questionnaires from my foster children. I did reserve tables and chairs to set up outside and the same company offered portable toilets. Having twelve foster children at the time and all the guests with children at the center, I went ahead and ordered six.

Eight

Avalina was twelve, but she was the size of an eight year old. Due to the fact that her parents were drug addicts, any time they were on a bender she would be locked in a linen closet in a hallway bathroom. Unfortunately, the only way she could fit, was for her to lay on the floor, in the fetal position, under the shelves. There were times she would spend weeks curled up on the floor. Once a day, her mother would toss in a few water bottles and a few snacks, if she remembered Avalina was in there.

A neighbor called in a welfare check when they realized no one had emerged from the home for several days. Police officers arrived and the front door was unlocked. Avalina's parents were discovered deceased on the floor of their living room from a drug overdose.

The police continued searching the rest of the home and found her in the closet, only wearing a diaper. The police thought she was a toddler due to her resemblance of a four year old. While she was recovering at the hospital, she revealed that she was, in fact, ten years old.

Avalina suffered from post traumatic stress and for two years she bounced around foster homes before social services contacted me. They felt as though she could thrive better at the recovery center. She had been doing pretty well and had latched onto Zarabella.

Zarabella was sexually abused by her father, beginning at the age of three. Her mother never wanted children because she didn't want to share her husband's attention. When her father began paying special attention to her, her mother began physically and verbally abusing her. In court, her mother claimed that she felt if Zarabella was injured, her husband would remain in their room for the night. Unfortunately, that never stopped him from sneaking into his daughter's bedroom.

When she was eight years old, her father would spend almost all night in her room. One morning, her mother violently attacked her and she was beaten so severely, her father had to rush her to the hospital. He played the doting father and explained his wife beat her. He was removed from the room in order for the medical staff to perform a full examination on Zarabella. That was when they had found she had also suffered at the hands of her father, not just her mother.

The hospital staff contacted the police and she felt as though she had been saved. She was able to record her statement for court, rather than having to face her parents again during their trial. After their sentencing, she was informed that her parents would be set free from prison at some point in her life. She didn't want her parents to ever be able to find her, so when she was ten years old, she requested a name change.

She wasn't given the name Zarabella at birth, it was the name she chose after social services and a judge accepted her affidavit requesting a name change. No one at the center, including me, knew what her birth name was and she wanted to keep it that way. Having Avalina to cling to helped both of them feel safe at night. If Zarabella slept alone, she would have a panic attack fearing that someone would sneak in and assault her. Avalina just didn't like being alone.

Zarabella was also lucky enough to have Kendall at the center as well. They were both thirteen and able to assist each other with their recovery, even though they grew up in very different households.

Kendall was a special case. Her parents waited until they were set with their careers and felt as though they were financially stable enough to have kids. Luckily, her mother had her eggs frozen in her twenties as a precaution. By the time they were ready to have kids, her parents were in their late sixties and they paid for a surrogate to carry Kendall.

By the time she was ten years old, she was basically taking care of her ailing parents. Within a year, a full time nurse had to come to their house in order to take care of her parents while she was at school. Due to their advancing age, they weren't able to give her the proper attention she needed once she hit her teens. Two months after her thirteenth birthday, her mother had a stroke and her father started showing signs of Alzheimer's. They were transported to a nursing home and Kendall was sent to the center.

When she first arrived, Kendall was bitter. She was upset that she wasn't able to spend quality time with her parents and she lost a lot of her childhood taking care of them. However, they had left her a pretty hefty inheritance. Her parents had issued one million dollars to the center in order to cover everything needed for Kendall to live there until she turned eighteen. Five hundred thousand was applied to pay for meals and housing, whereas the other five hundred thousand was to be used as spending money for her to spend however she wanted until she turned twenty one.

The day she turned twenty one, she would inherit another fifty million dollars. Kendall was basically set for life. She hadn't been at the center for long, but she also hadn't spent any of the money that was left for her. She was lucky enough to have Landon at the center when she arrived.

Landon was fourteen and he was an angry child when he had arrived at the center at the age of twelve. He had spent most of his life taking care of each of his parents. His mother lost a long battle with breast cancer. She was first diagnosed when he was three. It was caught early enough though that by the time he turned four, she was in remission. When he turned five, the cancer was back and she was so sick, she was bed ridden.

He wanted to spend as much time with her as he could, while he could. They had to hire a live in nurse to take care of her as her health continued to decline. She fought for her life until he was almost eight and lost. She took her last breath as Landon read a book to her.

She gasped for air, the nurse ran in and did what she could. Landon stood and watched as his mother lay lifeless in the bed she had spent the last year of her life. The nurse contacted emergency services and he watched as his mother's body was removed from the house.

His father fell into a deep depression and began spending more time on the sofa in front of the television. That was when Landon went back to taking care of his parent.

By the time he was ten, his father had quit working and Landon was no longer going to school. He was doing odd jobs for everyone in the neighborhood just trying to make enough money to pay bills. His neighbors noticed his struggle, realizing that his father was no longer going to work, some days they would call him over just to water their plants.

The female neighbors would make him lunch and sit and talk with him, giving him motherly advise and affection. The male neighbors would have him help them with fixing random things around the house.

One day when Landon left his father at home, so he could go to the grocery store, his father decided he could no longer live without his wife. Landon noticed his father was winding down in life and tried to shop quickly.

His Father left a note for Landon, ambled out to the garage and hung himself from the gears of the automatic garage door. He found his father swinging like a pendulum and called emergency services. The police turned him over to social services and the house was closed off as a crime scene.

Landon was held in a juvenile detention facility until the police cleared the scene as a suicide. One of his neighbors was given permission to escort him to his father's funeral. He was angry that he had worked so hard to take care of his mother before she was taken from him, then his father chose to leave him alone in the world. His mother had no choice, but his father made a conscious decision.

Landon was, however, able to connect with Griffon. Not only were they the same age, but Griffon lost both of his parents tragically. When he was seven, his mother decided to drop him off personally to school instead of him riding the bus. He said he was excited to talk to his mother on his way to school. She dropped him off, gave him a loving hug and he went on his way inside the building.

He was barely through the start of his school day when an office assistant entered his classroom. She whispered to his teacher, pointed at him, then escorted him to the front office where his grandparents were waiting for him. His mother had died in a fatal car accident on her way to work.

After his mother's funeral, Griffon and his father moved in with his grandparents and he became introverted. He spent most of his home time alone in his room and basically kept to himself at school. While his father was at work, his grandmother was taking care of him before and after school.

A few years later, when he was ten, his father was injured at work. He had fallen and hit his head on the concrete floor in the warehouse at his job. That time, Griffon wasn't escorted from school. He completed his school day as normal and was told by his grandparents that his father was in the hospital when he had arrived home.

His grandparents had been informed that the injury wasn't too bad and that he should make a full recovery. They were sure they had plenty of time to get there. After Griffon had completed his homework, his grandparents took him to the hospital in order to see his dad.

When they arrived, the three of them were told his father suffered a severe head injury and had slipped into a coma about a half hour before they had arrived. His grandparents allowed him to stay home from school as long as the school would grant the leave and send his classwork home each week.

One night, in the middle of the night, the phone rang. The hospital was calling to inform his grandparents that his father had died. He had never regained consciousness and as the neurons in his brain began to shut down, so did the rest of his body. Griffon was considered an orphan, but he was lucky to have his grandparents take him in.

His grandfather did everything he could to teach him basic life skills and his grandmother did everything she could to teach him how to take care of himself. Due to the fact that he excelled academically while he was doing his classwork from his father's hospital room, his grandmother decided to homeschool him.

He enjoyed the few years he was able to spend with his grandparents before they could no longer care for him. They had become frail in their old age and were unwilling to take what was left of his childhood from him by having him take care of them. That was when he came to stay at the center and brought a sweet chivalrous demeanor to the other boys.

Nine

Kensington on the other hand, had an extremely traumatic first few hours of life. Someone had dropped him off in a laundry basket at the front door of an animal shelter in the middle of the night. The umbilical cord and amniotic sack was still attached. He was crusted with amniotic fluid, which was assumed that his mother most likely gave birth at home, then packed him in the laundry basket and dropped him off within minutes.

When the owner of the animal shelter arrived the following morning, Kensington was crying and soiled without a diaper. The shelter owner called emergency services and requested an ambulance. She took him inside and wrapped him in a blanket. She didn't want to clean him up, so the medical techs and staff at the hospital could see the state that he was in. The shelter own-er was actually surprised he was still alive.

The ambulance arrived within minutes, followed by several police cars. The laundry basket was collected by the police and he was taken to the hospital to be exam-ined. During the examination, it was found that Kens-ington was born a month and a half premature with fetal alcohol syndrome and traces of heroine in his system.

Since he had come to stay with us, he had been happier and more willing to participate in activities. When he had first arrived, he sat in front of the recep-tion area, hugging his knees and rocking back and forth. I went over and sat next to him; silently at first, then when he stopped rocking, I introduced myself to him and asked if he wanted to see his new room.

I had already been told that he may have to stay in my room for a little while, so I had set up a small sleep-ing area in the room I shared with Jasper. He had turned toward me, touched my hand and stared into my eyes. I could see the hurt and abandonment in his eyes. I reached up and placed my hand against his cheek. He closed his eyes, took a deep breath and it was almost as though I could feel him relax.

When he reopened his eyes, there was a bond be-tween the two of us. It was as if he could see all the abuse I went through in my childhood and we were go-ing to help each other. I immediately knew that he was going to stay at the center and no matter what, I was going to protect him for as long as he needed me to. He only stayed in my room for about six months before he felt comfortable enough to join the other kids in the foster rooms.

Kensington's nick name was only for me. I called him my baby King, or my King. Using that name when he was upset seemed to give him confidence and calmed him down to explain what was wrong. If anyone else called him King, he would become absolutely outraged and aggressive. I loved him as though he was my own son and when he can gather his thoughts, he does call me mommy.

He might have been fifteen years old, but he had the emotional level of a six year old. His intelligence on the other hand, was off the charts. He was able to mimic the other children and no matter who he was talking to, he was able to change his communication to match. If he was playing with the younger children, he knew how to talk to them in order for them to feel as though he was their age and the same went for the older kids as well as adults. Everyone enjoyed having him there.

Kensington and Sawyer may have been the same age, but Sawyer knew who his mother was; his father on the other hand was a mystery. Sawyer was born to a teenage mother who refused to admit who his father was. Her father had died when she was young and they were very close. It really hit her hard and she had tried to find that same connection with all the boys she dated. She hid the fact that she was pregnant, at the age of fourteen, for as long as she could, until her mother pointed out that she knew.

When she found out she was having a boy, she felt as though she could recreate the connection she had with her father with her son. Unfortunately, she wanted to be his friend more than she wanted to be his mother. His grandmother felt as though she was having to raise him because his mother practically let him do whatever he wanted, even if it was dangerous.

Sawyer's mother was lazy and only wanted to spend time with him when she felt lonely. There were days she would push him away, wanting to be left alone and other days she would force him to cuddle with her when she needed the feeling of connection. She didn't want to discipline him because she didn't want him to hate her.

His grandmother knew he wouldn't be taken care of properly if she kicked him and his mother out of her house, but her health was failing around the time that he was eighteen months old. By the time he was two years old, his ailing grandmother died and his mother struggled to make ends meet. She would work at jobs for a few months, but hate the fact that she was being told what to do and would quit.

His mother was hardly around, but when she was around, she was loving and attentive. However, when she left to go to work, he never knew when she would be back. He never went to school and the most learning he received was from watching shows on the television, or his neighbor.

What Sawyer didn't know, was that his mother was a prostitute. She would rent a hotel room for several days at a time and have men come and go for days on end until she felt as though she needed to check on her son. She would spend a few days with him, then go back to the hotel.

For several years after his grandmother had passed away, his mother had been paying bills with money she was receiving for services rendered as a prostitute. She had been arrested for prostitution several times. Those were the times he would be left alone for weeks. As the years went on, she decided she could make more money by renting hotel rooms and booking appointments.

Just after his eleventh birthday, his mother had not only been arrested for prostitution, but also for possession with intent to distribute methamphetamine. Before social services showed up to take him into custody, she had been through a trial and sentenced to five years in jail. It wasn't until her sentencing hearing that she finally mentioned to her lawyer that she had a son.

He was walking home when he noticed the police presence around his house. Sawyer turned around and never went back. He lived on the streets for only a few weeks before he was spotted by a random good Samaritan who called the police. They had displayed a picture of him on the news that had to be a computer generated age progressed photo from the last photo that his grandmother had taken of him. The police picked him up and he was handed over to social services.

Due to the fact that he was extremely outspoken and opinionated, it was difficult to place him in a foster home. After being bounced around due to his harsh attitude, he came to stay at the center. When his mother still had approximately a year left on her sentence, Sawyer and I had spoken to her about how well he was doing at the center. She agreed to allow him to stay, as long as she was able to visit him once she was released.

He agreed and his behavior toward the other children changed. He became pleasant to be around and actually communicated with the older children, rather than screaming at them.

Sawyer and Archie were the two most independent children we had at the center. Archie was sixteen and came from a large religious family. He was the sixth child out of fifteen from his parents. His parents were devout Christians and deeply believed in the saying, 'spare the rod, spoil the child'. Each of the fifteen children were beat with an iron rod for any reason their parents felt was defiance, from the age of two.

When he was eleven and twelve, he would sneak out of the house on a regular basis. A few times Archie's parents would call the police and report him as missing. He would have to be gone for at least a month before they would notice, but being escorted home by the police was never a good idea.

His parents would explain to the police that he was a defiant child and a pathological liar. No matter what he told the officers on the way back to his parents house, his parents had already painted a negative picture of who he was and they wouldn't listen. He had tried to tell the faculty at his school, but his parents would explain it away. His friend's mother took pictures of his wounds and guaranteed that she would testify in court in his favor if he was able to get that far.

In the cases where Archie was brought home by the police, he would suffer a severe beating and would be confined to what his parents called 'The Naughty Room'. The naughty room was the storage closet under the stairs. There was a cot and a bucket for a bathroom, but nothing else inside the naughty room. There was a lock on the door and his parents would each wear a key to that lock around their neck.

Between the ages of ten and fifteen, Archie had run away from home so many times, he hadn't even realized his parents had three more children in five years. At that point, he knew he had to do something before the little ones began to suffer at the hands of his and his siblings tormentors.

The last time he ran away, he ran straight to the police station. He showed the police new and old wounds along with a crooked finger he had from when his father broke it and he wasn't taken to seek medical attention. An officer took him to the hospital and he received a full body x-ray. The x-ray showed several other broken bones that had healed incorrectly over time.

Archie had heard about the center opening while he was still in the hospital. A couple of nurses were discussing the center when they walked into his room to check his vitals. He asked them if they were able to put him in touch with Jasper and me. When we heard his story from the head nurse, we rushed over to visit with him in the hospital.

He told us the full story of his family and asked to come live at the center to recover from his traumatic childhood. He felt that if he went to live with his siblings, he would end up in jail. He wanted to live with us because he felt that he could be turned into a good person and the therapy could help him channel his anger.

We agreed and he became the first foster child in the center.

Archie and Finn only got along in group settings. They were the same age, but other than that, there weren't any other similarities between the two. Finn was dealt a bad hand in life. His father never wanted to have any children. When his mother revealed she was pregnant, his father told her to take care of it, or he would disappear and she would never see him again. She was excited to be having a baby and wasn't going to let his father take that away from her.

When he was born, his mother tried to be a good mother, but her mental health rapidly deteriorated. It started as postpartum depression, but as the months went on, she was spiraling. She wanted to take care of him herself, but when she imagined killing her baby, she realized she needed help. She wrapped him up, placed him on the floor of the passenger seat in the car and they moved in with his grandmother.

Around the time that he turned three, his mother began to lose her grip on reality. One night, his grandmother had walked in on his mother trying to smother him while he slept. She had been frustrated trying to potty train him.

When he was five, his grandmother admitted his mother into a mental health care facility so she no longer had to fear that her daughter could potentially murder her grandson.

His grandmother was granted full custody of him and took care of him up until he was thirteen. She was diagnosed with pancreatic cancer and he began taking care of her. He was fifteen when she died and he only spent a couple of months in custody of social services before he came to stay at the center.

It took quite a while for social services to find Finn's father. Once he was located, his father explained he didn't want to have anything to do with Finn. His father had grown a large company and had done everything he could to forget that he had a child out there, running around. He told social services that bringing a child into his home would ruin his social life and probably bankrupt his business.

At that point, social services decided he would be better off living at the center. We already had Archie by that time and we thought Finn would fit right in with him. We did what we could to make sure he felt welcome and included, just as we did for all of the other children when they first came to live with us.

Lily and Rose were identical twins. Along with their older sister Lavender, they were the newest of our foster children at the center. Their childhood wasn't filled with abuse, or neglect. They had loving parents, lived in a beautiful home, had friends that stayed over on a regular basis and because the three of them were so close in age, they enjoyed spending time with each other.

Their mother had started her own business and worked from home, their father was a marine and spent a lot of his time deployed in Afghanistan. When the twins were nine and Lavender was ten years old, their father was killed in action.

When the girls were fifteen and sixteen years old, their mother decided she could no longer care for her children - or possibly didn't want to - and she left the house. After a week, when their mother didn't return, Lavender called the police to report their mother missing.

She didn't realize that making a report would lead to the three of them being placed into three separate foster homes. When their social worker told them they would have to be separated, they came up with a secret meeting place the three of them would go to every time they were sent to separate homes.

At the point when social services could no longer find a foster home willing to take any of them, I was contacted with the request to house the three girls and I joyfully agreed. The first day they came to stay with us, Lavender was two weeks away from aging out of the system. Their social worker assured me I would only have to deal with them for a short time, then Lavender could request custody of her sisters from the court.

I sat down with the girls and explained that even when Lavender turned eighteen, they were all welcome to stay as long as they needed. I reassured them that no matter their age, they didn't have to leave until they were ready. She was free to live on her own once she became a legal adult, but unfortunately, she did not have the funds nor the means to live on her own.

Lavender appreciated the fact that we were even allowing the three of them to live together, that she became my helper around the center. I made sure all of the children knew they were welcome to stay at the center for as long as they needed and they all knew they had a place to come back to.

I wanted to keep my children safe at all times and since several of them were considered as a flight risk when they first arrived, they were schooled at the center. I wanted to be able to keep an eye on them and for those that were my extra special children, I wanted to be sure they wouldn't be bullied.

There was also the potential they could end up in a hostile situation that would cause them to react violently and I wanted to teach them the correct way to express their emotions. In my opinion, keeping a close eye on these children and teaching them how to take care of themselves in the outside world, was more important than sending them to a school where undisciplined and over-disciplined children would bully other children to make themselves feel powerful or important.

Ten

As everyone began to gather for dinner, I stood outside the dining area to greet each guest. As each one of my foster children entered the room, they embraced me before handing over their completed questionnaires. Every one of them seemed excited for the party, even the children who were usually sullen and mad at the world. I wanted to make sure they had a fun childhood before they grew up and had to become adults.

Kensington remained at my side as the guests filed in. Once everyone had been through the food line and taken their seats, I took Kensington's hand and wandered through the dining area heading toward the food line for the both of us.

I escorted Kensington over to the table with the other foster children before walking over to the table occupied by Charlotte, Jillian and Jasper and took my seat. It wasn't long before several of the ladies, who lived at the center with their children, approach my table. I stood up, so they weren't towering over me and I greeted them.

"Hello ladies. What can I do for you?" I asked.

"I hear you're having a party for the foster kids here at the center," Mary Hinson inquired.

Mary had been at the center for six months. Three months before she had become a guest, Mary was home alone with her two children, Charlie, seven and Marissa, five, when a man broke into her home, shortly after she had put her children to bed. The man tied her up, raped her and stabbed her five times. He thought she was dead and left her bleeding on the floor in her living room. She managed to get free and dialed emergency services.

"That is correct. This weekend I plan to have a party for the children that live here at the center," I told her.

"Is it for all of the children, or just your foster children?" Jenny Montgomery asked, with contempt.

"I'm not a cruel person. Of course it is for all the children. I'm just including the foster children in the planning. Everyone will be invited," I said, insulted.

"Well, it would have been nice to have been notified before we had to sit and listen to your children brag about the party you were planning just for them," Jenny complained.

"I don't have to explain myself to you, Jenny. You can leave whenever you want," I told her.

Jenny Montgomery was physically abused for years by her husband. Her three children - Jessica, twelve; Jasmine, ten; Jimmy, eight - all witnessed the abuse their entire lives. She had no control in her marriage, so after she came to stay at the center, she insisted on controlling everyone around her. She used intimidation and a threatening tone.

She had no problem scolding other people's children, but with her children, no one was allowed to say anything to them. She gave most of her attention to Jimmy, Jessica was forced to grow up too fast and Jasmine was mostly ignored.

Jenny insisted that her children agree with her no matter what she said. As long as they agreed with her and followed along when she harassed others, she was easier on them. Jenny acted like a mean girl in high school toward others and her kids were her lackeys.

"My husband hasn't been prosecuted yet, you know I can't leave. I need this place," Jenny said, her voice wavering as though she were going to cry, even though there weren't any tears.

She liked to go from the aggressor to the victim in the same conversation if she felt like someone was getting the upper hand on her. Most of the other guests tried to avoid her because no matter what they were talking about, she would try to turn the conversation to herself in order to get attention and sympathy from others. If the conversation wouldn't turn to favor her, she would hold a grudge against them and make up gossip.

To make matters worse, if she overheard other guests talking about her, or her children - even if it was innocent - she would tell her children they were bad people and the four of them would treat those guests poorly.

"Well, I guess you should change your attitude and get along with those of us trying to help you," I told her.

"Well, if we are done with Jenny problems, I would just like to say, thank you Mackenzie for everything you do for us and the children, here at the center," Mary said, touching my hand.

Jenny turned abruptly and stomped off to the table where her children were sitting. I watched as she gossiped with her children and pointed in my direction. All three of her children turned to look at me. I waved and smiled and they quickly turned back to their mother without acknowledging me.

Mary walked over to the table she was sitting at with her children when Jenny pointed at her and the three children glared at Mary's table. Mary and her children chose to avoid eye contact with Jenny, Jessica, Jasmine and Jimmy.

"Mackenzie said the party is for all of the children at the center. Jenny was overreacting again," Mary told the other ladies sitting at the tables around her, loud enough for everyone in the dining hall to hear her.

Once word got around the entire dining area, the guests and their children looked over at me, smiled and waved, happy to be included. I smiled and waved back, a little annoyed as I wanted the party to be a surprise and was trying to avoid the confrontation with Jenny, knowing she would overreact.

"I thought I told y'all to tell the kids this was a surprise. I didn't want anyone to know about the party before I passed out the invitations," I complained.

"We told them not to say anything to any of the guests, nor the children. Just because Jenny is a nosey bitch and overheard them talking, doesn't mean they said anything to anyone," Charlotte said.

"I guess I should have been more specific. Maybe next time tell them they can't talk about it at all? That way no one will overhear them and I won't have to deal with the bitchy mother," I said, shrugging.

As dinner service completed, the guests and their children began cleaning up after themselves in the dining area. As usual, Jenny and her children left their garbage and dishes on their table for someone else to take care of. Without speaking to anyone, they headed out of the dining area. Jenny, of course, held her head high, ensuring a posture to which could only be described as one of royalty.

"Are you going to help, Mrs. Montgomery?" I asked Jenny, as she walked passed me.

Jenny waved her hand at me as if to dismiss the fact that I had dared to even speak to her and her children grunted as they continued on toward their room. The adult guests disappeared into the kitchen area to wash dishes and clean up any left over food, while their children along side mine wiped down all the tables.

Jillian, Charlotte and I swept the floor under and around the tables to assist the children. Once my foster kids finished their chores, they ran over and surrounded me. All of them speaking at once.

"Hold on, slow down. One at a time. First, I have already ordered a bounce house and an inflatable water slide." The children erupted in cheers. "Let's go over and sit down in the therapy room," I said, leading the children toward one of the front rooms.

Eleven

The children positioned the chairs in a circle in order of their age. Avalina was to my right and Lavender was to my left. When the center opened, Jasper and I, along with Charlotte and Jillian, established a great rapport with child services. We attended certification classes to be sure we were equipped to accommodate a large group of foster children.

I started with Avalina. "Avalina, what else do you think I should get for fun for the party?" I asked her.

Smiling, she replied, "how about games?"

"Okay, what kind of games?" I asked.

As the other children glared at her and patiently waited for their turn, she immediately became apprehensive and looked down at her hands, as she shrugged her shoulders. She didn't like being the center of attention and she would become nervous in a group of more than three people.

When she squeezed her eyes shut, as tight as she could, I decided to move on to Zarabella. Avalina started trembling and whimpering as her anxiety began to rise to an uncomfortable level.

"That's okay Ava. I'll come back to you," I told her, in a soothing tone, which seemed to calm her for the moment.

Zarabella doesn't care for Gabrielle and tends to give her the most attitude. Several times, I have had to calm her after having a confrontation with Gabrielle. Zarabella doesn't like being told what to do, she prefers to be asked.

"Zarabella, what kind of games do you think we should have at the party?" I asked her.

"Can we do drinking games? With juice of course," Zarabella said, giggling.

"I second drinking games," Lavender chimed in.

"You'll have your chance, Lavender," I told her.

"That's right, save the best for last," Lavender said, smiling from ear to ear, as she leaned back in her seat.

"So, Zarabella, what kind of drinking games are you thinking about?" I asked.

"Beer pong, beertleship, word shots," she suggested.

I laughed at her innovation. "Okay, call me a fuddy duddy, but other than beer pong, what is beertleship and word shots?"

"Beertleship is like battleship, but your ships are set up as cups," Archie informed. "Anytime there is a hit, you drink the cup on that spot."

"That could get you trashed really fast, or keep you sober longer," Finn said, laughing.

"We are using juice, no one is getting trashed," I told them.

"Well, we can pretend," Lavender said, smiling.

"Moving on, what is word shots?" I wondered.

"You pick a word and every time someone says that word, everyone takes a shot, but of juice in this case," Zarabella explained.

"Okay, sounds like fun. Is everyone okay with these games?" I asked.

When Lavender, Zarabella, Finn and Archie stood up and began cheering loudly, Kensington came over and sat on the floor next to me, hiding his face in my lap. Avalina ran behind my chair and hugged my arm. I stroked Kensington's back, trying to calm him down and held Avalina's hand as she nuzzled her face into my neck.

"Okay, okay. Everyone calm down," I told them.

The noisy four calmed down and took their seats. Once the room quieted down, Kensington and Avalina seemed to emerge from their hiding places, but continued to cling to me. I was able to free my arm from Avalina and wrote down the game ideas with a safe twist. I knew these teenagers were troubled, but drinking games being suggested was funny to me.

"Alright, let's move on. Kendall, do you have anything to add?" I asked.

"Is it just for us, or are the other kids here at the center invited as well?" Kendall asked.

"I think it will be cruel not to include the other kids to join in. Everyone is invited, I just thought it would be fun to include y'all in the planning," I told them.

"Oh, good. Well, since there are some young children here, how about a piñata or a large ball pit?" Kendall suggested.

"That's sweet. Thinking of the other kids," I said. "I can do the ball pit, but I don't think giving some of the other kids a large stick to beat on something is a good idea."

The children all laughed and nodded, knowing which children I was referring to. Not only were Jenny's children questionable, but there were some that had their lives changed from accidental amputation and others who were just angry because their mother changed their living situation.

"Avalina, is there anything you want to add?" I asked, looking down at her next to me on the floor.

Her back was to the other kids, so when she looked up at me, she could only see me. I smiled at her as I noticed she had been crying. I was trying to reassure her that it was okay to feel overwhelmed and express her feelings. I leaned down and patted Kensington on the back. His head was still in my lap.

"My sweet King, may I sit Avalina in my lap? She seems upset and might need a cuddle," I requested.

Twelve

He sat up and I held my arms out to Avalina. She reached up and I lifted her into my lap. She curled into me, as I wrapped my arms around her, gently rocking. I decided to give her time to release her emotions before speaking to her.

"Okay Landon, you're up. What do you want to have at the party?" I asked him.

"I'm okay with what we have so far," Landon told me.

"There isn't anything you could think of that you might want to add?" I asked him.

"I can't think of anything right now," he answered, sullen.

"Okay, you think about it and I'll come back to you. Alright, Griffon do you have anything to add?"

"How about ring toss?" Griffon suggested.

"That sounds like fun," I said.

"If you get some two by fours and dowels, the boys and I can construct it and the girls can paint it," Griffon decided.

"That's a great idea. Is everyone okay with that?" I asked.

The others nodded in agreeance with the idea. Griffon was taught to build things by his father. His grandfather tried to continue on after his father's death, but his arthritis was too far advanced to do too much, so he was only able to watch Griffon.

"Kensington, I know you have an idea," I said.

"Alright my King, what are you thinking," I asked.

"I want bean bag toss," Kensington said, clapping his hands, rocking back and forth with excitement and laughing.

"You got it," I told him.

Due to his laugh being incredibly infectious, all the other children joined in with his excitement. The twelve of them stood up and began dancing around the room as Kensington belted out his favorite song. He would always sing when he was happy and his voice was amazing.

Lavender pranced over and grabbed my hands. She was trying to include me in their mini party. I stood up and swayed back and forth, allowing the children to play around. After a little while, the room began to spin around me, so I lowered myself back into my chair as I waited for the kids to return to their seats. It was about ten minutes before they decided they'd had enough fun and wanted to continue the party planning.

Kensington returned to the floor by my side, whereas Avalina returned to her chair between Zarabella and me. The girls held hands and whispered secrets to each other.

"Alright Sawyer, it's your turn," I told him.

"How about darts?" Sawyer said.

"We can do darts. You want a dart board?" I asked him.

"It depends. We may need to bring it inside, so the small children can't get injured," Sawyer suggested.

"That might be a good idea. Some of these small kids might run between the dart and the board. We don't need a young child running around with a dart sticking out of their head," Archie commented.

"Okay, we can put the dart board in here. Go ahead Archie, give me something else," I said.

"How about frisbee golf?" Archie suggested.

"That's interesting. I wonder if we would be able to set that up," I said.

"I can be in charge of finding an area to place it, if that helps," Archie said.

"That would be great Archie. Okay, you are in charge of finding an area to set it up. I will supply you with steaks and ribbon for you to mark where each goal will be placed," I told him.

"We can start with nine and if there isn't enough room for all of them, I will figure out the best placement," Archie began to plan.

"Okay, you plan it out and we'll all go shopping for materials for anything we will need," I told him. "Finn, do you have anything?"

"What about a small area for soccer?" Finn suggested.

"Okay Finn, you and Archie work together, so the frisbee golf and the soccer area don't interfere with each other," I told them.

Archie and Finn slapped hands in a high five and seemed genuinely in sync and happy to be working with each other. The two of them were genuinely like brothers. When they agreed on something they got along pretty well, but if they were left alone for an extended period of time they would argue.

"We got this," Archie said to Finn.

"We got this," Finn agreed with Archie.

"Good, now Lily, Rose and Lavender, the three of you have been over there whispering to each other for a while. What are the three of you thinking?" I asked.

"Lily and Rose, are there any games y'all would like to play?" I asked.

"I already seconded the drinking games. I just think that something a little stronger than juice might be more fun," Lavender said, laughing and nudging her sisters.

"Agreed," Lily and Rose concurred, simultaneously.

"Now Lavender, you know I'm not the one to contribute to the delinquency of minors," I told her, raising my eyebrows at her.

"Ooooooooooh," Archie and Finn mocked at the same time.

"Alright boys, that's enough. Girls, is there anything other than what has already been suggested that ya'll want?" I asked, rolling my eyes.

"No ma'am," all three echoed each other.

"Okay, thank you everyone. I appreciate your input. I will be planning out our course of action tomorrow and will request your assistance when Jasper and I are ready. Tonight, we have planned a special family movie night. Jasper is setting up cots with sleeping bags in our room and we will be having a slumber party. Go put on your PJ's and meet in my room in an hour," I told them.

My twelve children stood and danced around the room before approaching me. The girls came to me for hugs and the boys each gave me a high five. As a group, they left the room, while I sat for a few moments breathing. My stomach was feeling queasy and I was attempting to hide my ailment from everyone in the center.

Thirteen

The next morning, I attached my limb and quietly slipped out of bed. As I tip toed out of the room, I peeked at each one of my sleeping children. I decided to skip breakfast, but made sure to have my coffee. My stomach just wouldn't settle, so I grabbed a box of crackers to snack on. I spent most of the day in my office, organizing the event. I ordered the food, a ball pit, candy and party favor bags. I made a list of supplies for purchase in order to construct the setups for the other games.

Jasper and I were going to take the kids to the hardware store to purchase the supplies. I was glad that we still had a couple of days before the event, so I could get a handle on my tummy troubles.

We wanted the boys to grow up with basic handy-man skills, so they were going to put together all the games that required assembly. There were a specific set of skills we wanted the girls to grow up with, that also included them being handy, so they were going to paint what was assembled. We wanted the games to appear enticing, so I was going to let them pick out whatever paint they wanted that they found to be fun colors.

To ensure the boys wouldn't be using the power tools on each other, Jasper was going to assist the boys. Plus, some of the boys had never used power tools before, so he would have to teach them control. While all that would be going on, I would be assisting the girls. I figured I would mostly be overseeing them as they were decorating and painting.

The girls can become a bunch of little vandals if we allowed them to. I wanted to be sure that Lavender wouldn't try to convince the others to tag the walls in the therapy room. She was a sweet girl, but still needed guidance in life.

After lunch, Jasper and I piled the kids into the center's van and headed off to the hardware store. We split off as soon as we walked through the front doors. Jasper took the boys to the lumber area, while I took the girls over to the paint.

"Pick neutral colors that are fun," I told them.

"So, brown, grey and black?" Lavender said, slouching her entire body as low as she could go, while still standing.

"No, not just brown, grey and black. You can get yellow, green and different shades of red," I told her, mimicking her posture.

"What about blue? There are neutral shades of blue," Zarabella mentioned, pulling out a swatch card from the color wall.

"That's perfect," I complemented her choice.

"Okay, I get your point," Lavender said, straightening her stance and taking a deep breath.

The girls chose five different colors that they felt were fun and as neutral as they could find. The boys met us at the checkout with several different sizes and shapes of wood that none of the girls could figure out what they would turn into.

Once we were back from the store, I began feeling off; that was the only way I could describe it, off. All my energy was drained, I was out of breath just talking and felt like I just wanted to lay down and go to sleep. I didn't know why I felt so drained.

I did what I could to assist the girls with filling the party favor bags that had been delivered while we had been out. The boys were working diligently to get the games cut, sanded and assembled so the girls could begin painting. When Jillian came into the therapy room we were in, she must have noticed how lethargic I was. The girls were singing and had an assembly line going, placing items in the bags and passing them to the next person to do the same. I was sitting in a chair nearby, trying not to fall asleep.

"Hey, Kenzie. Are you feeling okay?" Jillian asked, placing a hand on my right shoulder.

"I don't know. I just feel absolutely drained," I told her.

"Maybe your body is finally relaxing after all the stress you have been through."

"It could be. You wouldn't mind staying with the girls, would you? I need to go lay down," I asked her, rubbing my forehead.

"No problem hon. Go ahead," Jillian told me.

"Okay girls, I'm not feeling well, so Mrs. Jillian is going to take over for me. Please be good and don't give her a hard time. I love you all," I told them.

Each one of the girls ran over to me for cuddles before I went to my room. I made it a rule that if anyone is not feeling their best and they voice their concerns, it would be a loving gesture to give them a hug and show them you are concerned.

The girls were only able to hug the other girls, while the boys were only able to hug the other boys. This was to ensure nothing inappropriate happened and it also protected them from false allegations. However, Jasper and I were both available for any child needing parental contact.

As I headed up the stairs, my depth perception was wavering. Each step seemed to be a different distance away from me. Some seemed far away, while others seemed so close. I caught my toe on the edge of a couple of steps and had to put my hands out in front of me to catch myself from smacking my face.

At the top of the stairs, I sat down for a moment to catch my bearings. My head was swimming and my stomach was flopping around like a fish out of water. I had just barely laid down in my bed for only a few moments before Jasper came in. He set a mug of steaming liquid down on the night stand next to me.

"Who is with the boys?" I asked him.

"Jillian is sitting with all of the children right now. She told me you weren't feeling well," Jasper told me.

"You left sweet, soft spoken Jillian with twelve children alone?"

"Don't worry. I asked Charlotte to go in and help her."

"Thank goodness. Those kids would take advantage of Jillian if they had the chance. So, what did you bring me?" I asked, slowly sitting up on the bed.

"It's peppermint tea. It will soothe your stomach and assist with your blood sugar if it's low," he said, handing me the mug.

I sipped the warm liquid. I could feel the cooling peppermint sensation trickle down my esophagus, into my chest and settle into my stomach. I knew it wouldn't help with the way I was feeling, but it was sweet of him to try to help, so I drank it anyway.

"What are you feeling?" Jasper asked.

"I don't know how to explain it. I just feel drained. It hit me hard and all at once. I think I'm just going to take a nap. I'll be up before dinner," I told him.

"Okay sweetheart. Hopefully you feel better when you get up," he said, kissing me on the forehead.

I took another sip of the peppermint tea, set the mug down on the nightstand and settled into the bed as Jasper left the room.

Fourteen

By the time I woke up, it was dark and Jasper was laying in the bed next to me…asleep.

'Shit, how long have I been asleep?' I thought.

I looked at the clock on my nightstand. The digital numbers showed me it was one thirty in the morning. That meant I had been asleep for ten hours. I understood why I was wide awake at that point. I swung my right leg off the edge of the bed and sat up. Reaching over, I grabbed my crutches, which were leaning against the wall between the bed and my night stand, instead of attaching my prosthetic. My left leg was leaning against the front of my night stand, but my bladder wouldn't hold off in the time it would take me to attach it, so I crutched myself to the bathroom.

Once I completed my business, I went back to sit on the edge of the bed. I picked up my phone off my night stand to scroll social media for a few minutes before wandering through the center. As the screen lit up, before I was able to enter my unlock code, I saw I had a notification from my text message app from Amber. Sliding the notification in order to open the message, I entered my unlock code.

'Mackenzie, I need your help. Angela is crazy. I'm being followed by a white panel van. Angela and her teenage son have threatened me. If I don't bring you to them, they said they would kill me. Please call me.'

I stared at the message for a moment, trying to figure out what I should do. Amber was informed not to contact me, but she had contacted me several times since she had left town. Since I had been ignoring her messages and phone calls, I decided I should probably respond to her that time. I knew it was probably not a good idea without consulting Faith first, but it was barely two in the morning and I wasn't going to bother her that early.

'Amber, I have already talked to Agent Leigh about your conversation with her. I know about Angela and her cult mentality. I recently came back from my honeymoon and am trying to live a semi-normal life. If you're having a problem, just move again. Go somewhere else and get away from Angela. That's all I can tell you for now. All correspondence after this should be done through Agent Leigh.'

I reread my response, then went ahead and sent the message. I didn't know how else to tell her nicely to leave me alone. Amber had deceived me and everyone else at the center. I preferred to avoid her and move forward with my life. I preferred avoiding Rebecca daily as well, because I wanted to put that part of my past behind me, but sometimes I would see her in the common areas.

Even though I was still feeling off, I decided I wanted to get up and start my day. I couldn't figure out what it was, but something was definitely going on with me. I thought I could be getting sick, but figured I would just wait it out since it just seemed to be nausea and fatigue.

I took a deep breath, reached over and opened the top drawer in my night stand. Grabbing my stump sock, I pulled it on and smoothed it out. As I grabbed my accessory appendage, I slipped it over the stump sock and strapped it to my thigh.

Slowly I slipped out of bed and ambled over to my closet. After getting dressed, I quietly left the room. I made my way down the stairs and to my office in order to finalize the activity list for the afternoon.

Once I had the party completely organized, I made my way into the kitchen for coffee. Since by that time, it was four in the morning, I figured some of the parents would be getting up soon, so I set one percolator to brew a full carafe.

As I waited for the coffee to brew, my phone rang. I pulled it out of my pocket and looked at the screen. It was Amber. I slid the bar at the bottom of the screen and answered it.

"Amber, you need to stop calling me," I told her, after putting my phone up to my ear.

"Mackenzie, please. You don't understand. We are both in danger. Angela told me there were four people that came into contact with you on your honeymoon. They were there to abduct you, but Jasper was always around. They are now keeping an eye on you. Agent Leigh needs to be informed in order to keep you safe," Amber said, with a panicked tone.

"What are you talking about? Why should I believe you? You took me out into the middle of nowhere and I was almost murdered by our father. Why would you care if someone wanted to kill me now?" I wondered.

"I saved you, remember."

"Saved me? Saving me would have been stopping Brett Carter from reopening my amputated stump. Saving me would have been not allowing him to give Rebecca an identical amputation. I now have to put up with her daily."

"Just keep your eyes open for four people you met on your honeymoon. They could at any time show up and you can't fight off four people on your own. Also, Jasper is not who you think he is. Just tell Agent Leigh what I told you. She can keep you safe," Amber said, before hanging up.

"Wait! What do you mean Jasper is not who I think he is? Amber?" I yelled into the phone, after the call had disconnected.

I put my phone back into my pocket and thought about Sara, Dustin, Hallie and Camden. They seemed like normal people, other than the fact that they annoyed the shit out of me. Not only that, but what did she mean when she said Jasper is not who I think he is? Was Amber implying something negative about my husband, or was she just trying to scare me?

Fifteen

I filled a travel cup with coffee, added a little creamer, pressed the lid down on top and headed back to my room. I wanted to talk to Jasper about the four people we had met on our honeymoon. I didn't get the vibe that they were stalking us, just a few coincidental meetings. I was going to sit in the chair next to the window and wait for him to wake up.

I slowly turned the knob and tried opening the door quietly, but that caused the door to create a loud groan. Jasper rolled over in the bed and opened his eyes, peering in my direction. I froze in the doorway waiting to see if he was going to wake up, or close his eyes and go back to sleep.

He blinked several times as if he was trying to figure out if he was dreaming. When he lifted his head up and squinted his eyes as the light beamed in from the hallway, I knew he was waking up. I stepped into the room and closed the door.

"What are you doing?" he asked.

"I can't believe I slept as long as I did. I missed dinner. I just went out to organize the day's events and get some coffee. Amber contacted me again. It started as a text exchange, but while I was waiting for the coffee to brew, she called me," I informed him, as I walked over to the chair in front of the window and sat down.

He sat straight up in bed and turned on the bedside lamp. "What did she say?"

"She told me that the two couples we met on our honeymoon were there to abduct me for Angela. Luckily, we were always together so they were unable to fulfill their task. She also said they are going to continue to attempt to abduct me, so I shouldn't be left alone."

"Are you talking about the four people we came into contact with the first few days of our honeymoon and never saw again?"

"She didn't mention them by name, but I'm sure that's who she is talking about."

"Well, do you think she is telling the truth?" Jasper inquired.

"There is no way she would know anything about Angela. I only spent one night in that foster home. The second night, the foster mother beat me and I needed medical attention. We all escaped and were scattered from there. I never saw her, or any of the other children from that home, again. I didn't even think about her until Faith told me about the conversation she had with Amber," I told him.

"I remember you telling me about Angela when we were kids and we were sharing stories about our past foster homes. Are you sure that you didn't possibly share that information with Amber during a conversation when she was pretending to be mute?"

"I haven't even thought about Angela in years. She wasn't exactly a significant part of my past."

"Are you sure? When you first moved into the group home with me, you seemed pretty sure that the kids from your first foster home were the ones who helped you get through all the shit you went through."

"What are you even talking about? Why does it sound like you are trying to defend Angela's actions? Just because they gave me advise when I was six years old, doesn't mean they helped me through anything. As a matter of fact, Angela wanted me to keep my mouth shut about our abusive foster mother and just comply with the bitch's orders. If anything, the boys helped me more than Angela did," I argued.

"Okay, okay. So, do you know what happened to Angela when y'all were split up?" Jasper inquired.

"Well, according to Faith, Angela and Gwen were sent to live with an overly religious family. The couple who adopted them, preferred adopting siblings because, according to them, it helped the children acclimate to their new surroundings if they had someone else there they were comfortable with."

"That makes sense. How many kids had that couple adopted and over how many years? Do you know?"

"I have no idea. Faith didn't tell me and I didn't ask, but what she did tell me was that the family that adopted them was actually part of a polygamist cult. They brainwashed the children into believing they were existing in a more meaningful life and everyone in the compound was family."

"How was a polygamist cult able to adopt so many children?"

"They weren't technically doing anything illegal. They only had one marriage that was recognized by the state. The other marriages were only recognized by their church," I explained.

"They aren't really much of a family if they are living a polygamist lifestyle. It would be mostly incest, right?" Jasper wondered.

"Not necessarily. The women were ordered to have one child each year until they could no longer reproduce. After that, they would have to adopt two or more children each time one is married off. Most of the biological children were arranged to be married to the adopted children."

"So, every time one child in the house is old enough to be married, each woman in the house hold adopts two or more children?"

"Something like that. I guess that's their way of growing the compound with fresh members, rather than converting adults who could potentially run off and spread lies."

"How old are the children when they are married off?"

"Angela was eighteen when she married one of the elders and when Gwen turned eighteen, she married the same guy."

"How many kids do you think are in the same house at one time?"

"I'm sure that they have between ten to fifteen kids, per mother figure, at one time in each house. In reference to that, it depends on how many wives the guy has."

"You think those people we met on our honeymoon are her children?"

"I think they are members of the cult, not necessarily Angela's children."

"Did Amber tell you what Angela wants with you?" Jasper quizzed.

"According to Faith, Amber told her that Angela wants me to join the cult. She thinks I'm marked by the devil and I need to be saved before I end up with the devil's spawn. Her words, not mine," I informed him.

"Why would Angela be interested in you now, years later, if y'all haven't seen, or spoken to each other since you were six?" he asked.

"There are a lot of reason's I can speculate, but I'm not sure exactly."

"Well let's start with one reason and I'll try to find a loop hole."

"Okay, well number one, she told me to keep my mouth shut about the foster mother and not talk about the abuse, but the other children wanted out. She was only bitter because she didn't want to be separated from

Gwen. She was bonded to Gwen and felt the need to protect her," I told him.

"Technically you didn't say anything, right?" he asked.

"Not really. I just got mouthy with the foster mother until she beat me so badly the other children helped me run away and we all were saved from the home."

"But they weren't separated."

"No, they went to the same house."

"So, what's another one?"

"Well, the foster home they were sent to was part of a cult. What if she is bitter about the whole cult thing and now she wants revenge?"

"Yeah, I guess I could see why she is mad at you. You sent her to go live with a cult. That's it, you're screwed. There's nothing we can do," Jasper said, sarcastically.

"Alright, well I guess I should just give up and go with her," I said, laughing. "But first, I need to lay down for a minute."

All of a sudden, the room felt as though it were swirling around me. I started seeing black spots and my stomach felt as though someone was jumping up and down on it like it was a trampoline. I stood from the chair and began stepping toward the bed. My equilibrium was off, so I fell face first onto the mattress and slid down the side of the bed and onto the floor.

Jasper quickly sprang up out of bed and immediately scooped me up into his arms and placed me in a lying position on the bed. I laid as still as I could to avoid the spinning feeling.

My husband placed his hand on my forehead as though he was checking to see if I had a fever. He pulled his hand away, lightly pressed his lips to my head, then walked over to the dresser to put on a shirt and change out of the shorts he wore to bed.

He chose a pair of his casual shorts, then decided on an outfit for me. He retrieved one of my camisoles and a pair of my sweat pants in order to assist me with getting dressed easily. Placing the clothes for me on the foot of the bed, he walked over to the large oversized chair to put his socks on.

"Mac, sweetie, I'm going to help you change out of your night clothes and I'm going to take you to the hospital. Are you okay with that?" Jasper requested my consent.

"Is it absolutely necessary for me to go to the hospital?" I asked, confused.

"Yes, it's necessary for you to go to the hospital. You weren't feeling right yesterday, you slept for ten hours and now you practically passed out. We are going to catch what is wrong with you early before it gets any worse."

"I guess, but I didn't technically pass out because I didn't lose consciousness," I told him.

I felt as though everything was happening in slow motion as he removed my pajama pants and slid on my sweat pants. I barely moved as he tried to dress me.

"Are you able to sit up to change your shirt?"

"Possibly with assistance. Just be slow about it."

Jasper placed one hand on the back of my neck and slowly assisted me to sit up, bending at the waist. My body felt heavy and my hands, foot and back were tingling. The black spots in my line of sight had been joined with white spots and they danced in my vision.

At that point, I don't remember my shirt being changed, or being taken out to the car. The next thing I remember was opening my eyes and seeing Jasper standing over me with a huge grin on his face. I looked around and realized I was lying in a hospital bed.

"What happened?" I asked Jasper.

"Well your eyes were open, but you were unresponsive when I was changing your shirt. I was able to get you into a standing position and helped you to my car. By the time we made it to the hospital, you were completely out and I had to have a nurse bring out a wheel chair to help me get you inside," he explained.

"Okay, so why are you smiling so big? What is wrong with me that you think is so funny?"

"Well first, they were able to determine you were dehydrated, so they attached a line of fluids. They also believe that what you were experiencing was a stress related panic attack, but there is something else they were able to find," he said, with a bounce in his step as he rounded the bed to the other side.

"Oh my god! What is it?" I insisted.

"You're pregnant!"

"Wait, what?" I said, the corners of my mouth curled up and the muscles in my cheeks tightened.

Jasper wrapped his arms around me. My heart felt so full, tears emerged from my eyes and rolled down my cheeks.

"It's still early, so we have to keep it to ourselves for a while," Jasper informed me.

"How the hell am I supposed to do that? I have to tell Jillian and Charlotte and I want to inform Faith," I said.

"Okay, slow down. First of all, the doctor said that you are still in the miscarriage window and it is hard if you tell people too early, then have to go back and tell them you lost it."

"Wow, way to ruin a mood."

I went from excitement to an intense feeling of fear. I placed my hands on my belly and remembered the sadness when I had lost my twins. I knew they had been conceived from hateful and sick reasons, but they were growing inside me and I felt a connection with them. I may not have really wanted the twins, but this baby was made from love and I wanted this baby.

"I can see the hurt in your eyes. I know what you are thinking about. Don't think about it too much. Just take care of yourself and the rest of us will keep you safe from danger. Nothing unnatural will happen to our baby," Jasper assured me.

I didn't mention what Amber had said to me about Jasper to him, because I wanted to hold on to that information. Knowing that if I talked to him about our past, I would be able to come to my own conclusion of whether or not he is who I know him to be.

Sixteen

The hospital staff forced me to eat and drink at least two bottles of water before I was released from the hospital to go home. I wanted to be excited about the baby, but with all the tragedy I had faced, it was more fear than excitement.

When we arrived back to the center, Charlotte and Jillian were waiting in the reception area with the foster kids. The kids ran up to us and the fourteen of us embraced as a group.

"Are you doing okay?" Lavender asked.

"I'm okay. I was just dehydrated and hungry. I do think I would like some tea though," I said.

The children all ran off to the kitchen. I stepped up to the reception desk to get closer to Charlotte and Jillian.

"I have some news," Jillian said.

"Why didn't you say anything before? We have been standing here for over an hour waiting for them to get back and you didn't tell me about any news," Charlotte pouted.

"I wanted to wait for Kenzie and tell you both at the same time," Jillian informed.

"Okay, just tell us what it is," I said.

"I'm pregnant," Jillian said, beaming.

"What? That's wonderful," I said, wrapping my arms around her neck and biting my lower lip.

"Okay well, for me it's still a little early, but me too," Charlotte announced.

The three of us just sort of stared at each other for a moment, as if they were waiting for me to reveal some big news as well. Seeing as Charlotte and Jillian had just announced they are pregnant together, I figured I might as well chime in with my news.

"Ladies, me too. I was overworking my body and not drinking enough water. Plus, I had slept through dinner last night, so I was hungry and with the little person inside me taking all my nutrients, I passed out. I was informed at the hospital," I said, beaming at them both.

Charlotte and Jillian squealed like teenage girls at a boy band concert. As the children emerged from the kitchen I tried to shush my sisters. I didn't want my foster children to know about the baby yet. Lavender walked up to me and produced a cup of tea.

"Thank you. I really appreciate it," I said, taking the cup from her and sipping.

"You weren't supposed to say anything yet," Jasper said, as he stepped up behind me and wrapped his arms around my waist.

"I know, but I couldn't help it," I told him.

"What happened?" Kendall asked.

"Nothing sweetie. Hey kids, how about y'all go outside and play while the grown-ups talk," I requested.

"Yes, let the grown-ups talk," Lavender said, shooing the kids toward the door.

"Lavender, you too," I said, as she turned back to join us.

"I'm eighteen. That means I'm now one of the grown-ups," she argued.

"I would agree with that normally, but I need to discuss something with my sisters before I discuss it with you kids, okay?" I told Lavender, as gently as I could without invalidating her feelings.

"Fine, but can we discuss my place here at the center later? I would like to be treated more like an adult with y'all, rather than being lumped in with the other children," Lavender huffed, before walking away.

"I'm just shocked that the three of us are pregnant together. Isn't that exciting?" I said, leaning back against Jasper's chest.

"How far along are you?" Charlotte asked.

"Medically speaking, four weeks. Scientifically speaking, two weeks," I said, rolling my eyes.

"I know what you mean. I don't understand how they can start from before conception if the baby didn't technically start forming until two to three weeks after their start day, but whatever. This is so exciting," Jillian said.

"Technically, each month is one cycle. That cycle begins and ends in twenty eight days for most women. You have nine of those cycles when you are pregnant and out pops baby," Charlotte explained, thankfully G rated as the children came running into the room.

"It doesn't matter. We are having a party today and things are going to start getting delivered soon. Let's get ready to have some fun," I said, changing the subject, so the children didn't hear our conversation.

I was only hiding the fact that I was pregnant from my foster children because I wanted to approach the subject gently. Not wanting any of the children to feel as though they were being replaced, I wanted to sit down with them and answer any questions they might have.

"A truck just showed up with the bounce house," Zarabella said, jumping up and down in front of me.

"That means it's almost time. Y'all go upstairs and change into something to go down the water slide in," I told them.

The children cheered and rushed off upstairs to get ready for the planned festivities. I stayed behind with Charlotte, Jillian and Jasper. I wanted to know how close together our pregnancies were.

"So how far along are you two?" I wondered.

"I'm eight weeks," Charlotte said.

"I just hit twelve weeks," Jillian said.

"Each of you are still too early to be announcing your pregnancies," Jasper pointed out.

"I couldn't hold it in anymore. I wanted to tell my sisters," Jillian said, tears pooling in her eyes.

"I wanted to share after Jillian said something and I'm pretty sure Mackenzie felt the same way after the two of us spoke up," Charlotte told Jasper.

"Okay well, I'm going to leave you ladies to talk about baby stuff. Don't forget about the party," Jasper said, kissing me on the cheek, then heading up the stairs.

Jillian, Charlotte and I stood in the reception area clucking like high school girls about how fun it was going to be with the three of us pregnant at the same time and having our babies close together. Charlotte struggled with infertility for years before pushing the stress aside and deciding if it happens, it happens. Jillian and Mark wanted to plan it out with charts and statistics along with a baby budget. Jasper and I weren't even sure I could get pregnant after Malachi cut the twins out. Either way, the three of us were so happy to be able to share this special milestone in our lives.

Seventeen

When the caterer showed up for the party and several other vendors where right behind, Charlotte and Jillian escorted them to their staging areas, as I went upstairs to change my clothes. When Jasper and I came back down to the reception area, most of the guests, along with their children, were creating a bustle in the front of the center. I realized there were four mothers surrounding my twelve foster children, who were huddled together in a group.

Jenny was wagging her finger as she was practically towering over the young children. Lavender stood between Jenny and the other eleven children, in attempt to shield the others from the poisonous words coming from the woman's mouth.

"Excuse me. What is going on here?" I asked Jenny, as I stepped between the children and the venomous hate.

Kensington wrapped his arms around my waist, resting his head on my shoulder, trembling. I wrapped my arms around his shoulders. Jasper requested the three other women to join him over near the reception desk.

"Your rejects were talking about how the party was for them and no one else was invited. I was just setting them straight," Jenny spat.

"We never said anything like that. We were talking about the activities and how much fun it was to plan and choose what we got to do," Avalina explained, with tears streaming down her face.

"Jenny, I'm sorry, but I'm going to have to ban you from the party," I told her.

"Ugh, mom," Jenny's children wined, simultaneously.

"Jessica, Jasmine and Jimmy are all welcome to join us because I don't believe in punishing the children for their parents actions. After the party, you and I will be discussing whether you are able to stay here," I told her.

I turned my back toward Jenny and began ushering the children out toward the garden area where the bouncy house was being set up. Jenny didn't appreciate what I said to her, so she felt as though she needed the upper hand and shouted at me.

"Don't worry, I will be gone before the party is over and my kids will not be attending," Jenny said, grabbing her children and pushing them up the stairs.

Her three children argued with her about how unfair it was that they wouldn't be able to participate and she yelled, "life isn't always fair," as they went into their assigned room.

I took the children into one of the therapy rooms. "What happened?" I asked them.

"We were sitting at the bottom of the stairs talking about how much fun it was to help plan and prepare for the party when Jenny and her kids were coming down. Jenny told us it was rude that we felt the need to brag about getting a party just for us when there are other children at the center. When I started explaining to her that the party was for everyone, she started yelling at me that I was being disrespectful and just because we were rejects and didn't have a real family, we should still respect grown-ups," Lavender explained.

"We are your family, for all of you. Jasper, Charlotte, Jillian and I are all your family. And none of you are rejects. We chose each and every one of you to be in our lives. Jenny has had a life filled with people telling her what to do. We need to be understanding of her situation, even if we don't understand her actions. I will talk to her and make sure she understands that she cannot speak to any of you that way again, so none of you have to endure her hate speech. I love and adore you all in your own unique ways and hope you all continue to grow into the wonderful adults I know you can be. Were any of the other ladies saying anything to y'all that upset you, or was it just Jenny?" I reassured my foster children.

"The other ladies were trying to stop her. Mary Hinson was the first to come over and tell her to stop," Lavender told me.

Most of the girls were crying and the other children were doing their best to comfort them. Lavender was visibly shaken by the interaction, but being the oldest, she was holding it together pretty well.

"Well let's not let one person ruin our day. If anyone needs cuddles or just wants to talk about what happened, both Jasper and I are here for you for anything you need," I told them, with Kensington still holding on to me for dear life.

Avalina and Zarabella were the first two to come over to me for cuddles and reassurance. Kensington stepped around behind me, his arms still wrapped around my waist, but my arms were free to hug the others. I was kind of hoping that Jenny would still be around after the party so I could discuss with her how inappropriate her actions were.

"I know," Zarabella whispered in my ear, before placing her hand over my abdomen.

Zarabella glared over at Avalina. Avalina kissed me on the cheek, wiped the tears from her face and skipped off to join the other children. I turned in order to spin Kensington back around to in front of me, before sitting down on a chair in the room. I brought Zarabella over and had her stand in front of me next to Kensington.

"My sweet King, is it okay if I have a moment alone with Zarabella? I promise Lavender will keep you safe while I'm not with you," I asked, nodding at Lavender who stood in the doorway.

"Okay mommy," Kensington agreed, before slowly stepping toward Lavender, but continuing to look over his shoulder at me.

"What do you know?" I asked Zarabella, after Jasper had ushered all of the other children out of the room.

"I know about your baby. I'm happy for you and Jasper to have your own baby," she told me.

"How do you know about that?" I asked her, wondering if she had a special psychic ability.

"I over heard you with Mrs. Charlotte and Mrs. Jillian," she said, smiling from ear to ear.

"You little sneaky snake. Do the other kids know?" I wondered.

"Nope, your secret is safe with me, until you tell them of course," she said.

Zarabella grabbed my hand and pulled my arm for me to stand up. I stood and she led me out to the gardens where the party was set up. The other children were already playing. She walked me over to where Jasper was standing, let go of my hand, wrapped her arms around his waist and hugged him. When she pulled away, she smiled up at him, then waved at us before running off to go play with the other children.

"Hey, it's so great to see the children having fun," Charlotte said, as her and Jillian approached.

"We had a slight hiccup this morning, but I think everything is okay now. Unfortunately Jasper, we may have to set up the bed in our room for Kensington tonight. Jenny's actions today may have caused a set back," I informed them, as we walked over and sat down.

"Oh no, what happened?" Jillian asked, concerned.

"Jenny Montgomery happened," I said.

"Oh good grief. Was she bullying the kids in order to make them feel bad about themselves so she could feel superior?" Charlotte questioned, rolling her eyes.

"Isn't that what she does?" I said.

"Exactly, no one can measure up to how perfect her spawn are," Jillian commented.

"Even though her children are just as vicious and vindictive as she is," Charlotte added.

"Children only mimic what they see. I feel bad for them since their only role model is a raving bitch," I said.

"I think that woman is a twat," Charlotte said, using her colorful words.

"Can we please be a little less vulgar when there are children present," Jillian requested, wrapping her arms around her belly.

"Your baby still has a tail. I'm sure it can't hear yet," Charlotte told her.

"Okay ladies, calm down," a small voice said from behind us.

We turned to see Matthew Kirkland approaching. The three of us applauded as he strutted toward us.

"How is my favorite little man?" I said, as he hugged me.

"Well, you know, living the dream of being surrounded by beautiful women," he said, making his way around the table.

For only being five years old, Matthew was pretty suave and debonaire. We believed he was an old soul due to his demeanor and some of the things he said.

"Looking good ladies. Keep it up," he said, before heading over to join the other children in the bounce house.

Most of the other guests had come out to join us with their children. Shortly after the interaction with Matthew, Kensington came running over to me, crying. At first I thought he had fallen and hurt himself, but once I realized he didn't appear injured, I was concerned.

"My baby King, what's wrong?" I asked him, as he fell into my embrace.

All he did was point in the direction of a group of kids. My foster children were standing in the middle of a circle with other children from the center surrounding them. There were three children in particular that were being overly aggressive.

"Jasper, can you please go find out what is going on over there?" I asked him, as Kensington attempted to climb on my lap like a toddler.

Jasper sauntered over and a couple of kids tried to run off, but Tom and Mark walked up with Jasper and stopped them from fleeing. As the men talked to the group of children, they began allowing the children to run off to play except the three who were being aggressive. Jasper, Tom and Mark perp walked the three children over to me. Once they were close enough, I was able to see they were Jenny's kids.

"Kensington, what happened?" I asked him, cupping my hands around his face, as the men brought up the three children.

"Them mean," he said, burying his face into my neck.

Kensington, being fifteen, was having a difficult time trying to curl up on my lap. Whenever he was upset, he wanted to sit in my lap as I held him. The poor sweet boy just wanted to feel love and acceptance and I was willing to make sure he got what he wanted. He wouldn't be able to climb up into my lap when I would be in my third trimester, but I'm sure that the two of us would figure something out. I know that Kensington would probably live at the center his entire life, but I hoped that he would grow out of his phase of climbing into my lap.

"What are y'all doing here? I thought your mother was packing all of you up to leave?" I wanted to know.

"Our mother told us we could come out here while she figured out where we would go from here because you were kicking us out," Jessica said, with her arms crossed over her chest, as she rolled her eyes at me.

"I am not kicking y'all out. I just told your mother that if she is unhappy here at the center, she can leave whenever she wants," I told her, as I rocked back and forth with a very upset Kensington on my lap.

"That's not what you said. You told her that you wanted to talk to her about leaving," Jasmine snapped at me.

"Look, I'm not going to discuss that with you children, but if you don't have a place to go, y'all are more than welcome to stay here. There is no reason for the three of you to bully the other children. If I have to, I will separate you three from your mother and y'all will not be able to communicate with each other. It is very apparent that your attitude is based on what your mother tells you. How about the three of you become your own people and stop allowing your mother to control your opinions of others. Now, if you three would like to join in with the other kids and have fun, you are more than welcome to. If you cause any more trouble, you will be told to go to your room," I informed them.

"You can't punish us," Jimmy mouthed off.

"Try me," I said, raising my eyebrows at him.

The three of them just agreed after that and ran off to join in the fun. I patted Kensington on his leg and he stood up off my lap. He understood that he was too big for me to hold him for too long, but his attachment to me would create a toddler mindset in him when he was upset. He sat down on the ground in front of me and placed his head in my lap.

"Are you okay now sweetie?" I asked him.

"I okay. I stay here, or go play now?" he said.

"My sweet King, if you want to go play, you can go play," I told him.

He stood up and ran off, heading over to where his foster siblings were playing. Tom and Mark joined us at the table, while Jasper slipped inside. I didn't know where he was going, but he was free to go inside if he wanted, so I didn't think anything of it.

"We are going to need to talk to Jenny. She can't keep telling her kids bad things about us, then expect to continue to live here. Of course we aren't going to force them out onto the street either," Jillian said.

"I will contact a few shelters to see if they have room before we tell her she needs to go. I couldn't live with myself if I thought those kids were living in her car," I told them.

"Those kids are assholes, but of course having an asshole for a mother doesn't help," Charlotte chimed in.

"Charlotte, you can't blame the children when the mother is the one causing them to act the way they do. Jenny is the main contributing factor for her children's attitude toward everyone. She is the reason Jimmy takes things from the other children, then walks away proud of himself," I told her. "I'm sure Jenny is a narcissist."

"Jessica is getting to that age where she will start to influence the younger two just like her mother. I wonder if she does the same thing with family members?" Jillian said,

"You think Jenny talks shit about her family to her kids?" Charlotte asked.

"It could be possible. Why would she come to the center instead of going to stay with family when she left her abusive husband?" Jillian commented.

"That's true. When she first got here, didn't her mother and sister visit? It was sparingly, but they visited. Now they don't come by anymore. Of course, a narcissist prefers others to be miserable in order for them to be happy," I commented.

"That's right. I remember her sister saying, 'good luck' one time on her way out shortly before her mother left," Jillian said.

"Sounds to me as though she is just an all around problem," Charlotte said.

"That's all we need is another Wendy Mason," Jillian said, rolling her eyes.

"Better that than another Amber," Charlotte told us.

"Amber has been contacting me," I told them.

"What the fuck?" Charlotte said.

Just before I was able to explain, Jasper had returned and a few of the mothers came over to our table.

"Thank you so much for doing this. The kids are having a great time," Mary Hinson told me.

"You are so welcome. The kids deserve a little fun," I told her.

"Can you please talk with Jenny's kids. They are harassing and bullying some of the other children," Georgina said.

Georgina was twenty four with an eighteen month old little boy named Georgie, when she tragically lost her husband. It became a domino effect of loss. She lost her income, she lost her home and her husbands family basically cut her off from the family. Her husband's family was trying to take Georgie away from Georgina once she became homeless.

She was assigned a social worker in order to assist her with being able to keep her child while she mourned the loss of her husband and basically her lifestyle. We took her in at the center in order to protect her and her child from living on the streets.

"Again? Guys, you're up," I told them.

Tom, Mark and Jasper stood up and headed out to find the trouble makers.

"I am so sorry. I had just spoke to them when they were causing trouble with my kids. They are going inside now and we won't have to worry about them again," I reassured them.

"Is there any way we can have a center meeting with all the grown-ups and talk to Jenny? That way we can voice our concerns directly to her," Mary suggested.

Jasper, Tom and Mark arrived with Jessica, Jasmine and Jimmy in tow. The three children were protesting about being pulled away from the fun.

"What did I tell you three not even an hour ago?" I asked.

"Look, when one kid is going to act stupid, we are going to call him out on that," Jasmine responded, folding her arms across her chest.

"Yeah, you gotta tell them they're stupid because they are too stupid to know they're stupid," Jimmy said.

"Shut up Jimmy. You're stupid," Jessica joined in.

"Okay, that's enough. This was supposed to be something fun for you kids, but the three of you are making it difficult for the other children to have fun. The guys are going to escort you to your room and talk to your mother about your behavior," I told them.

Mark, Tom and Jasper took the children inside and the other mothers thanked me, then walked away to watch their children. I turned back to my sisters who were keeping an eye on Kensington. He was sitting in the grass with Avalina and Zarabella. The three of them had a ball from the ball pit they were tossing back and forth.

"I love how sweet those three are to each other," Jillian said.

"They are the most sibling like of the bunch. Other than Lily, Rose and Lavender of course," Charlotte said.

"One good thing about all the foster children here, is that they look out for each other," I said.

A shrill scream came ringing out from inside the center. Jessica, Jasmine and Jimmy came running out with the three guys trailing behind.

Eighteen

Charlotte, Jillian and I stood up and stepped up to our husbands. The three children fell to the ground, crying, as they huddled together.

"What happened?" I asked Jasper.

"You need to call Leigh," Tom said.

"What happened?" Jillian repeated.

"We will take care of this. Y'all go do what you need to do," Mary said, walking up with three other moms who crouched down next to Jenny's children.

Charlotte, Jillian and I rushed inside behind Tom, Mark and Jasper with the guys several steps ahead of us. They stopped outside of Jenny's room, waiting for us to catch up. Once we were standing with the guys outside the closed door, Jasper prepared us for what we were going to see.

"It's not as bad as Wendy, but it's bad," Jasper said, before turning the knob and swinging the door open.

Jenny Montgomery was hanging from a rope that had been coiled around the ceiling fan and tied to one leg of the foot of the bed. The other end was tied into a noose and wrapped tightly around her neck. There was bruising around her neck, her eyes were frozen in a look of terror, lips had turned blue and she had been disemboweled. Her end trails had been pulled completely outside of her abdomen and piled neatly on the floor, just below her swinging corpse.

"Please tell me the children did not see this," I said, as my legs buckled underneath me and I fell to the floor sobbing.

Tom shut the door as Charlotte and Jillian screamed, turning away from the gruesome sight, and into the arms of their husbands. Jasper knelt down next to me and wrapped his arms around me in comfort.

"Just a quick glimpse before Mark stepped between them and the scene and shut the door," Tom said, as he embraced his sobbing wife.

"Okay, wait," I said, wiping the moisture from my face with my shirt.

Jasper assisted me to my feet. Tears continued streaming down my face, as well as Charlotte and Jillian sobbing uncontrollably. I was having trouble gathering my thoughts.

"This is a crime scene. We need to keep the guests and Jenny's children away from it. I need to call Faith. Someone help me call Faith. She will know what to do," I said, shaking, sniffling and trying to blink away the tears.

I pulled my cell phone out of my pocket and handed it to Jasper. He dialed the number saved into my phone under Faith's name. Jasper turned and walked away in order to get away from the sound of Charlotte, Jillian and me sobbing uncontrollably. The three of us embraced.

"How could this have even happened?" Charlotte wondered, placing her hand over the lower half of her face, tears moistening her cheeks.

"I can't even figure out how someone could have done this without anyone noticing," Jillian mentioned, with one hand placed across her forehead.

"The person who did this would have been covered in blood as they left. That is, if it was an outsider and not someone who lives here at the center," Mark said.

"Even if they live here at the center, the person who did this would have been covered in blood," Tom corrected.

"I know that, but they wouldn't have been caught leaving covered in blood. If someone who lives here at the center did this, they would have been able to clean up before being seen, which means it will be harder to find the suspect," Mark clarified.

"Alright, Faith says that everyone needs to get away from the room. Y'all head back out to the party and Mackenzie and I will meet y'all out there later," Jasper told them, ushering my sisters and their husbands away from the room.

Jasper wrapped his arms around me, trying to help calm me down. It wasn't helping due to my hormones on high alert, but I appreciated the comfort. I felt as though Jenny's children could be traumatized by the sight of their mother's swinging body.

"I have to go. We need to get away from the room. I can't stand here any more," I told Jasper, pulling away from him and rushing down the stairs to the reception area.

Jasper slowly stepped down the stairs, as I again fell to the floor in front of the reception desk. I placed my hands on the floor in front of me and began hyperventilating. As Jasper rubbed my back, I gagged several times before the entire contents of my stomach decided to evacuate.

After heaving several times, I leaned back and sat on my foot, with my prosthetic straight out in front of me, wiping my mouth with the back of my hand. My face throbbed and I was breathing heavily, as Jasper walked toward the front doors to wait for the police.

The center security guard, Damion, stopped the golf cart he was driving at the front doors. Damion stood at six foot two inches and had a rippling body. He approached me when we were preparing the center for guests and asked to be the security guard. We took him to the police station and had a full background check done and he was completely clean. He's a single man whose mother raised him and his brother right. Damion worked fifteen hour shifts of his own accord and the over night shift is handled by his brother, Derik, who is basically built just like him. He noticed Jasper standing there and saw me on the floor with a puddle of vomit in front of me.

"Is everything okay?" Damion asked, as he poked his head into the center.

"The police are on their way. We have had an issue inside the center and have had to contact the authorities. When they arrive, will you please direct them inside?" Jasper said.

"I can do that," Damion told Jasper, before turning toward me. "Are you okay, Mrs. Tully?"

"She's fine, we just had a situation. Do you know who that van belongs to?" Jasper asked.

"I've never seen it before," Damion responded.

"What van? Where?" I asked, standing.

I rubbed my face with my hands, took a deep breath and walked over toward the front doors. I peered out into the parking lot and spotted the white paneled van at the far end.

"I've been keeping an eye on it. It parked there a couple of hours ago and I haven't seen anyone get in, or out of it," Damion said.

I will stay here and keep an eye on the van. I'll do my grounds check after the police arrive," Damion said.

"Thank you Damion. You are definitely a valued member of the faculty, here at the center," I told him.

"Would you like me to contact the housekeeping company to have someone come out and clean up the front reception area?" Damion asked.

"No, thank you. I will take care of it," I responded, turning and heading toward the janitorial closet.

"I will be right here out front if you need anything Mrs. Tully," Damion said.

"Like I said, she's fine. Just send the police in when they get here," Jasper said, walking away from the front doors.

Jasper headed upstairs as I proceeded to mop up my vomit off the floor in front of the reception desk. From the time that Jasper and I got married, he seems to have changed. Charlotte and Jillian had noticed it before the honeymoon and I had definitely noticed it as soon as we got back.

Once the reception area was clean and I returned the mop and water bucket to the janitorial closet, I stepped down the hall where the door to the party was located. We wanted to make sure none of the guests from outside were coming in to peek at the body.

"We might want to hire a couple more security guys to have one out front and one walking the grounds all the time. It's a lot of pressure to have one during the day and one at night. The building is too large to only have one security guard to patrol each one of the doors through a twelve hour period. Certain entrances are unmanned more times than they are being watched," I suggested, when Jasper met up with me down the back hallway.

"Well, considering we now have two bodies on our roster, we probably should hire more security," Jasper agreed. "What do you think would be the best? Just one extra during the day and one extra at night?"

"I'm wondering if it would be best to hire three more for during the day and three more at night. That

way, we have four security guards at all times, but I believe it would probably be best to get Damion's opinion
about the extra guards. Unfortunately, if history repeats
itself, whoever is behind this will come after me next,"
I said.

"You shouldn't assume that this is a warning for
you, besides, I'm not letting you out of my sight until
this baby is born. I saw the underlying message, don't
get me wrong, but no one besides your family knows
you're pregnant. There's no reason to assume the worst,
but stay on guard," Jasper reassured me, wrapping his
arms around my waist.

"I'm only taking this as a warning because of what
Amber said. Plus, that white paneled van is what she
told me was following her," I explained.

"You think the people in that van are here to abduct
you?"

"I don't know, but I'm more afraid now that I'm
pregnant to be alone for any reason. I hope Faith gets
here soon," I said, as we headed back up to the front of
the center.

As soon as I spoke, we saw several police cars and
Faith's unmarked FBI vehicle swung into the parking
lot and stopped right outside the front door. They exited
their vehicles, some leaving their car doors open. I was
thankful they didn't have their sirens blaring so they
wouldn't alert any of the guests at the party.

I watched out the window as Damion approached
several officers and motioned toward the van in the far
back corner of the lot. Faith, along with several other
officers, rushed straight to the front doors.

"Holy shit Mackenzie, are you alright?" Faith asked, the second she was through the door.

"I'm okay, for now. This is horrible, especially for her children. Oh no, I need to contact her mother and sister. Hopefully, they will be willing to take Jenny's children," I said, as Faith embraced me.

"Who all has seen the body?" Faith asked, as she pulled away, but held my hand.

"Jenny's children were bullying the other kids, so Tom, Mark and I were taking them back to their room to be dealt with by their mother. That's when we found her. We brought the children back outside and took Charlotte, Jillian and Mackenzie to see," Jasper explained.

"Why would you take them up to see the body? It's a crime scene, not a side show. Did anyone go into the room?" Faith wanted to know.

"No, we only stood in the doorway. We immediately removed the children from the scene and no one else wanted to compromise the crime scene," Jasper told her.

"Can you show me to the room?" Faith requested, kissing the back of my hand, then leading the way upstairs.

"I'm going to have Jasper take you to the room and I'm going to check on everyone outside. I just want to make sure that Jessica, Jasmine and Jimmy are okay," I said, letting go of her hand on the third step.

"Wait, take an officer with you. I don't want you to be alone," Faith suggested, concerned.

"I'll be fine. I'm just going out that door, right there. You can see the door from where we are standing," I said, pointing down the hall.

"Kenzie, there are three other doors down that hall where someone could be hiding. They could just pop out and grab you," Jasper voiced his concern.

"You don't want to alarm the guests. Jasper you take her outside and make sure there are people with her, then come back. I'll wait," Leigh said.

Nineteen

As Jasper escorted me back to the party, he interlaced his fingers with mine. I kissed the back of his hand as we approached the door.

"We will get this taken care of. Stay with Charlotte and Jillian. I will come back as soon as everything is being investigated and Faith no longer needs me," Jasper told me, before giving me a kiss and heading back inside to meet back up with Leigh.

"What's going on right now?" Charlotte asked.

"The police and Faith are here. How are Jenny's children?" I asked.

"Distraught, what happened? How did someone get in and out of the center without being noticed?" Jillian wondered.

"We aren't sure yet, but it seems we have another Wendy event," I told them, sighing heavily.

"Is everything okay?" Mary asked.

"There isn't a lot of information I can give you right now, but thank you so much for keeping an eye on things while we dealt with the situation inside. I will make a statement later," I told her.

I rubbed my face with my hands after Mary and the other ladies had walked away. Grabbing a chair, I placed it next to Jenny's kids. They were huddled together on the ground next to the table and I felt as though I should talk to them. I gathered my thoughts before saying anything.

"Hey, I'm going to be contacting your aunt and grandmother. Jessica, did you want me to do it, or did you want to call and talk to your grandmother?" I asked Jenny's children.

"I don't want to talk to her. This is her fault anyway. I would rather stay here," Jessica said, tears streaking her face, as she stared down at the ground.

"Why would you say what happened to your mother was your grandmother's fault?" I wanted to know.

"When we left my father's house, my mother tried to go to my grandmother's house, but she refused to take her in because of us," Jessica said.

"Are you sure that's right? I don't think your grandmother would have said that," I told her.

"Are you saying my mother is a liar? How dare you!" Jasmine yelled, through her tears.

"I never said your mother was a liar, I just think she may have misunderstood," I tried to reassure them.

"I don't know why you would even call my aunt Courtney. My mom has always said she was a bitch who never liked us anyway," Jessica told me.

"I don't like it when you use that language, Jessica," I said.

"I don't care what you think. There isn't anyone in our lives anymore that actually gives a shit," Jessica cried, wrapping her arms around her siblings.

I took a deep breath, stood up, looked at Charlotte and Jillian, pursed my lips, raised my eyebrows and shrugged. I moved the chair back over to the table.

"Okay, well I need to go make this phone call, but I have been advised not to go anywhere alone," I stated, peering at Mark and Tom, as they stood behind their wives.

"You want just one of us, or both?" Tom asked, changing his stance as if he were about to fight someone.

"Well, I would only need one, but if you two need to do everything together, I could use you both," I said laughing.

Tom and Mark slapped their hands together in a high five, as I stood up and turned toward the door in order to head inside. We walked toward my office, so I could make the call.

The police presence in the center was thick and most of the officers were just standing around watching the doors. I stepped into my office and sat down behind my desk, while Tom and Mark stood outside the door. I pulled up Jenny's emergency contact information, picked up the center phone on my desk and called her mother. Susan answered the phone on the second ring.

"Hello?" Susan said.

"Hello Susan, this is Mackenzie Tully from The Ansley Kirkland Center for Recovery. We have had an issue with Jenny this afternoon. Are you able to come to the center so we can talk?" I asked her, with a somber tone.

"Of course. Are the kids okay?" she asked.

"I would rather not discuss this over the phone. The kids are physically okay. Are you able to contact Courtney, or did you want me to do that? I think you should both be here."

"Mackenzie, you're scaring me. Is it really that serious?"

"It really is."

"I will pick up Courtney and be there as soon as I can," Susan said, before hanging up the phone.

"Hey Tom," I called out, from my seat.

"What can I do for you?" Tom said, as he entered my office, while Mark stayed outside the doorway.

"I need to figure out the best way to handle this situation with Jenny's mother and sister. Are you able to find Agent Faith Leigh? I would like some advise on what to say to them," I requested.

"You got it Mackenzie," Tom said, as he stepped out of my office in search of Leigh.

Mark stood outside my office, Tom ran off upstairs toward Jenny's room and I sat staring at my desk. If what happened to Jenny was a warning to me, how long would I have to wait before they came after me? I didn't want to have to look over my shoulder for months worrying about when it would happen.

"Mackenzie, you wanted to talk to me?" Faith said, interrupting my thought.

"Hello Faith, I need your advise," I told her, as I stood.

"Sure, what can I do for you?" she asked, stepping into my office and sitting down on the sofa.

"First, we may need to get some items for the children from that room. Do you know how long it will be before we can do that?" I inquired, stepping over to the sofa and sitting next to her.

"I'm not sure. They are collecting evidence, taking pictures and they will need to remove the body, before you will be able to go into that room. If I have to, I will go out and buy some clothing for the kids," she said, touching my hand.

I nodded, looking down at my lap, as Jasper entered and stepped up behind me. I was so glad he was there; I needed his support as well. Jasper slid his leg up over the arm of the sofa and leaned across the back behind me.

"Is Tom and Mark still out there?" I asked Jasper.

"No, I told them to go back outside to take care of their wives," Jasper said.

"I hope you didn't say it like that," I told Jasper.

"It was something like that. I'm sure that Charlotte and Jillian would prefer to have their husbands out there with them. You were suppose to be outside until I came back to get you," Jasper said.

"I came inside to call Jenny's mother and sister, so they could come here in order for me to inform them of the incident. I'm not sure how to approach this situation. I was just wondering if Faith had any advise on what I could say to them when they get here?" I requested.

"That's fine," Jasper said, standing and moving over to one of the chairs across from my desk.

"Okay, the first thing you're going to want to do is make sure they are calm. Don't give them too much information. Just tell them she was alone in her room and she was found deceased," Leigh informed.

"Should I tell them that her kids saw her like that?" I wondered.

"How are the kids? Jasper told me about that."

"They are traumatized. I don't want Jessica, Jasmine and Jimmy to go home with their grandmother, or aunt and tell them what they saw. I think it would be shocking if Susan or Courtney were caught off guard finding out that those poor children saw their mother hanging from the ceiling fan with her intestines on the outside of her body."

"Your right. You don't want the new guardian to be caught off guard when the kids describe what they saw. The best thing to say is the children discovered their mother and the center staff was able to remove the children quickly," Leigh explained.

"Do you think you could be in the room with me when I talk to them? I'm afraid of what might happen if the situation gets out of control," I told her.

"I will sit on this sofa in the back of the office and let you handle it. If they seem to get out of hand, I will step in. Jasper should also be here in case they ask any questions about the discovery of the body," Leigh said.

"That sounds good. I can do that," I said. "Jasper, are you okay with that?"

"I'm not going anywhere," Jasper said, as an officer peeked his head into the door and knocked lightly on the doorframe.

I stood up and walked over to my desk, as Leigh shifted on the sofa. Jasper walked over behind my desk and stood behind my chair. I sat down and leaned forward against my desk.

"Yes sir, what can I do for you?" I asked.

"There are two ladies here to see you," the officer told me.

"Please send them in," I said, leaning back into my seat.

"Mackenzie, what is going on?" Susan asked, as she and Courtney walked through the open door.

"Please, sit down," I said, as Jasper walked over and closed the door.

"What did Jenny do now?" Courtney scoffed, as they sat down.

"We have had an incident involving Jenny. She had been alone in her room. Her children were being escorted back to the room when she was found deceased," I started to explain.

The two of them stared at me, dumbfounded. Susan's eyes widened, her face began changing to a pinkish hue as tears rolled down her cheeks. I gave them a few moments for the information to sink in before I continued.

"I'm so sorry for your loss." I hesitated before continuing, trying to be as gentle in my wording as possible. "At this point, I am thinking about Jessica, Jasmine and Jimmy. They are going to need a place to live and I feel like family would be the best for them," I explained.

"How did she die?" Courtney asked.

"There aren't any specifics as of this time, but they are in there now investigating," I said.

"So what can you tell us?" Susan asked, wiping the tears from her face.

"The children were there when she was discovered, but the center staff was able to remove them from the scene quickly," I recited exactly what Leigh told me to say.

"How did they find her?" Courtney wanted to know.

"That's not important. What is important is that Jessica, Jasmine and Jimmy are going to need a lot of support from the two of you," I continued.

Jasper quietly stood behind me with one hand on my shoulder and Leigh was only spectating from the sofa. Susan placed her head in her hands and sobbed as Courtney rubbed her back.

"Can we see the children?" Courtney asked, without any emotion.

"Of course. Did you want me to have them brought in here, or did you want to go to them?" I asked.

"I don't want to be in this office anymore. Take me to them and Courtney, why can't you show that you care, even just a little?" Susan said, rubbing her face.

"Okay, everyone is outside today. We were having a party for all of the children here at the center," I informed them as we all stood and headed for the door.

Jasper and I led Susan and Courtney down the hallway toward the exit, as Faith headed up the stairs to return to the crime scene.

"She was a horrible sister and has never been nice to me. I hope you are able to get the kids to understand that we were never the problem," Courtney told Susan.

"Courtney, your sister has just passed. Be respectful," Susan scolded Courtney.

"Fine, whatever," Courtney huffed, shrugging.

"Now, if the kids were outside, why was Jenny in her room alone? Are the adults not invited to the party?" Susan argued.

"Jenny was probably being a bitch and stomped off to her room to pout," Courtney said.

"Your sister has just died. Show some respect," Susan scolded Courtney again.

"Sorry momma. I'm sorry Mackenzie. Go ahead," Courtney said, rolling her eyes before lowering her head.

"She was being disrespectful this morning to some of the guests and I told her that after the party I wanted to discuss her continued residency here if she was going to be disrespectful on a regular basis. That was due to an incident from a couple of nights ago as well," I explained.

"See momma, I told you she was being a bitch," Courtney said.

"That's enough out of you," Susan scolded Courtney, a third time.

Twenty

Jessica, Jasmine and Jimmy were sitting at the table with Charlotte and Jillian when we came out. They didn't even notice Susan and Courtney at first. It wasn't until we were closer to the table when Jasmine looked up.

"Gigi," Jasmine said, bursting into tears and running into Susan's arms.

Jessica and Jimmy followed behind their sister to hug Susan, leaving Courtney standing with Jasper and me, off to the side, forgotten.

"Once the police and coroner are done in the room and they have taken Jenny to be examined, we will make sure their stuff gets packed up. Courtney, if you would like to come back into my office and sign all of the necessary paperwork, we can discuss the arrangements for the children. We will need to talk to social services about the best placement for them, to ensure they aren't separated into foster care until the investigation with what happened to their mother is completed," I explained.

"What do you mean? Why would we need to talk to social services about the best placement for the children?" Susan asked, still clutching Jenny's children.

"I need to contact social services before they leave to go live with anyone. They will make sure the right person receives custody of the children. Also, I can help make arrangements for the funeral," I assured her.

"I want to go live with dad. Mom hasn't let us see him since we came here," Jimmy said, pulling away from Susan.

"We just want to make sure you are safe," I told him.

"My dad never hurt me. He loved me and taught me stuff. My mom always told us bad things about my dad, but I knew it wasn't true," Jimmy said.

"Maybe we can talk about having a visit with him," Susan told him.

"I would rather live with Gigi," Jessica said.

"Me too," Jasmine agreed.

"Dad never hurt us," Jimmy said, stomping his foot.

"No Jimmy, dad never hurt you. You were lucky enough to be born a boy and you never dealt with him being angry. Dad thinks all men are superior to women and we should just do what we are told without question. He just let you run wild and do whatever you wanted, while the rest of us just had to do what we were told, or face the consequences," Jessica informed.

"I would rather stay here at the center if everyone is going to fight over us. Is that okay Mrs. Tully?" Jasmine asked.

"Well, for now I think it would be best if you three stayed here. Just until I speak with child services. I would like to request though, that you not bully the other children," I told them.

"If they aren't coming with us, then why did you want us to come here?" Susan asked, standing up straight and crossing her arms over her chest.

"I thought it would be best if you heard the news in person, rather than over the phone. Also, I figured you would want to see the children and make sure they were okay. Their mother has just died and they are going to need support from everyone in their lives right now. I also think it would be in their best interest to stay here and participate in the group therapy sessions," I explained.

"I would rather take them home with me and schedule therapy for them. They would be better off with me anyway," Susan stated.

"I'm willing to live by the rules of the center if it means the fighting stops. We have listened to our mother trash everyone in our lives for as long as I can remember. I have never actually seen the actions from these people, that my mother has told us. I would like to be able to form my own opinion about everyone. Mrs. Tully and everyone here at the center has always cared for us, as well as the other children, no matter what my mother told us," Jessica stated.

"Why don't we go back to my office and discuss this," I told Susan, before turning to the children. "If the three of you want to go play for a little while, we will be right back."

"I also want to talk to that FBI agent that was in the office with us," Susan said, before turning and storming into the center.

Twenty One

Courtney and I followed Susan into the center and back to my office. I was not willing to allow these three children to leave the safety of the center to potentially end up in the home of an abuser. There wasn't anything that could stop their father from getting custody of them at that point.

"If their father has abused those girls, it would not be advisable to allow any of them to leave the center," I told them, once the door to my office was closed.

"Look, if my daughter would have died at home, the police would let me take the children. So tell me, why *you* won't let me have them?" Susan said, emphatically.

"First of all, if Jenny was murdered at home, social services would take the children for a couple of weeks, while the police continuously questioned them. Then there would be a hearing as to the custody of the children. If it was determined that their father didn't kill her and he has the means to support the children, he would be awarded the children. It's within the best interest of the children to keep them here at the center. If you take them home, their father has the right to come to your home and take them with him. With that, you have no legal leg to stand on because he will be awarded the children for the pure fact that he is their biological father. I'm sorry, but if you want legal custody of the children, you have to leave them here until after they talk to social services," I explained.

"The children are safe here, mom," Courtney said.

"Okay, I see your point. Am I at least able to visit them?" Susan asked.

"You can come visit anytime. I'm sure they would enjoy that," I reassured her.

"Alright, let's do this. What do we need to do right now?" Courtney asked.

"I have standard enrollment paperwork, which basically allows the children to school here at the center with the foster kids. That way we can guarantee that their father can't withdraw them from school and take off with them. I also have a temporary custody agreement that is only for medical purposes if they were to get sick, or for any reason have a medical emergency," I explained.

"Will I be contacted if there is a medical emergency?" Susan wanted to know.

"Absolutely, I will be sure to contact you once there is a diagnosis for whatever is ailing them," I told her.

"Why would I have to wait until they have a diagnosis? You wouldn't tell me immediately that they have a medical emergency?" Susan asked.

"Once there is a diagnosis, there is more information I can give you. If they are sick, would you want me to call and tell you they seem to have a cold, but I haven't taken them to the doctor yet? Wouldn't it be easier if I could call and tell you they have a viral infection, then let you know what medication they are taking? I said, condescendingly.

"She's right, you know?" Courtney said to Susan.

"Fine, I understand," Susan said, taking a deep breath.

I pulled out all the required paperwork for Susan and Courtney to both sign. I wanted to be sure they were giving me and the staff at the center temporary custody of Jessica, Jasmine and Jimmy. I knew the three of them would not be happy that they would have to change rooms, but considering their status had changed, they would have to move in with the foster kids.

"You are both welcome to stay and join us for the afternoon festivities if you like," I told them.

"That would be great, thank you. I would appreciate being able to spend time with my grandchildren that my daughter kept from me for so long," Susan said, as we stood and headed toward the office door.

"Can I say something without you getting mad at me?" Courtney asked Susan, as she stopped in the front reception area.

"As long as you aren't going to just say that Jenny was a bitch," Susan told her, rolling her eyes.

"No, I just want to say that I think Jenny was a narcissist and she was only happy when others were miserable. It was only a matter of time before she pissed off someone just enough," Courtney said, shrugging.

"God Courtney. You never have a nice thing to say about your sister," Susan stated.

"How can I say something nice about someone who was so inherently selfish, that she had purposely kept her children away from family, in order to control their perception about said family. She liked to tell lies to others in order to gain sympathy for herself. I literally thought she was injuring herself, then turning around and claiming her husband was beating her. I thought she was lying for sympathy. That was until the girls started getting random injuries.

"I told her she needed to leave her husband in order to save her children. For years she told me that she was the only one in danger and the only reason the girls got hurt was because they got in the way when he was beating on her. She told me Jimmy knew to stay out of the way. When I tried to talk to Jessica, Jenny kicked me out of her house and blocked me from being able to contact her, or her children.

"She knew they were in danger, but refused to protect them. I fault her, just as much as I fault her husband. She shut everyone out of her life, those of whom she couldn't manipulate. She then, convinced her children that anyone she couldn't manipulate was a bad person and they couldn't be trusted. I believe Jimmy is the narcissist in training and we need to do what we can to reverse it, before he embraces it," Courtney explained.

"Why had you never told me any of this before?" Susan asked.

"Because you won't listen to anything negative said about your oldest daughter. Jenny has mentally and verbally abused her children since they were about a year old. Once she could manipulate them mentally, that's when she started breaking down their spirit, so they would have to depend on her for the rest of their lives," Courtney said.

"That can't be true," Susan said, her legs buckling under her.

"It is true. You just couldn't see it because you are her mother and she was just that good as a manipulator. Since she grew up in your house, she knew what to say and how to say it, in order to get you to feel sorry for her. She made you think that she was a better person, than she really was. Jenny had treated me like shit my entire life. It never really started to click that she was a narcissist, until she would go years without talking to me. I started to realize, it was because my life was happier than hers and she didn't like that. She was only happy if others around her were just as miserable as she was. I refuse to allow life to define who I am and do what I can to enjoy life to the fullest," Courtney said, as we assisted Susan into the chair behind the reception desk.

"I feel so blind sided that I didn't realize that my child was callous and calculated," Susan said, sobbing uncontrollably.

"Jenny was a cold hearted bitch and I feel as though this could be seen as a good thing. She is no longer available to leak her toxic behavior onto others," Courtney said.

"That's awful. Could you please be a little more courteous. Despite the fact that you wrote her off as your sister years ago, I did just lose my daughter," Susan scolded Courtney, as she wiped her face and nose with a tissue.

"Well, I love you mom, but you would never listen if anyone spoke ill of your golden child. I tried to tell you several times about Jenny's behavior, but you would just tell me to stop. That bitch made my life miserable and lied about me to her children. Then she would spend years not talking to me because I refused to wallow in self pity with her. Plus, I refuse to allow her to manipulate me into thinking that her life is so bad," Courtney argued, with Susan.

"I'm done having this conversation. Take me out to go see my grandchildren," Susan said, standing.

Quietly, the three of us walked back outside to be with the children. Jasper was standing just outside the door, waiting for me. We sat at the table with Charlotte, Jillian and their husbands, while Susan and Courtney sat at an empty table.

Twenty Two

Once I was twenty weeks pregnant, Jasper and I headed off to receive the gender ultrasound. Both Charlotte and Jillian already knew the gender of their babies, but they were waiting to reveal what they were having until Jasper and I knew what our baby was.

We were still awaiting more information from the murder investigation of Jenny. Faith told me that the medical examiner had found Jenny's killer had also given her a complete hysterectomy. Her uterus had been found mangled inside the pile of her intestine. The forensic lab was still running tests to find any evidence of another person. So far, they had only been able to find DNA from Jenny and her children in that room.

"Are you excited?" Jasper asked, once he had parked the car at the doctor's office.

"I don't know if I want to know. I feel as though it might be more exciting when they announce it after the baby is born," I told him.

"It would be easier to buy things for the baby, once you know. It will help you relax. You have seemed so tense since we found out you were pregnant."

"I'm terrified because what if the same thing happens with this baby that happened with the twins. I didn't know the gender of the twins, but it makes this baby more real once we know the gender."

"The baby is real regardless of knowing the gender. Also, do you really think that someone is going to cut you open and try to take our baby?"

"You never know. Amber was telling me about Angela stalking me and then the Jenny situation at the center. I'm just saying, it's a possibility."

"At this point, you are just grasping at straws," Jasper told me, rubbing his forehead.

"Okay fine, let's go in and find out what we are having," I said, reaching for the car door handle.

Jasper reached over and touched my hand. He smiled, grabbed my hand and kissed the back of my fingers. I smiled back, then we exited the vehicle and headed toward the front door of the medical plaza.

We checked in at the front desk, then sat down to wait for my name to be called. I cried quietly, stared at the ceiling, with my hands clutched between my knees and my legs jiggled. It didn't take long before the inner door opened and a nurse holding a medical chart emerged.

"Mackenzie Tully," the nurse called out.

Jasper and I stood up and followed the nurse into the hallway. She stopped at the scale and I stepped on to be weighed.

"You must be eating very healthy. You have only gained two pounds since the last time we saw you. Good job, mommy," the nurse said, as I stepped down off the scale.

She then directed us into the sonogram room. Jasper sat down in the chair next to the exam table, as I climbed up onto the exam table and lay down. I pulled my shirt up over my growing belly and the nurse tucked a paper bib into the waistband of my pants, then squeezed the warm jelly onto my abdomen.

"Okay, do you want to know the sex of your baby?" the nurse asked, as she ran the wand over my belly.

"Yes, we do," Jasper chimed in.

The nurse looked down at me and raised her eyebrows, questioningly. I silently nodded and she nodded back.

"It's a girl," the nurse announced.

"We're having a girl, Mackenzie," Jasper told me, standing up and kissing my forehead.

I did feel a little better, knowing that I was having a girl. I felt as though I could raise her to be loving and caring. I didn't know how I would feel if I were having a boy. I did know that I would worry every day if he would one day grow up to be angry and aggressive. I have had experiences with all kinds of boys growing up and it just seemed as though eventually, boys just become aggressive. Matthew seemed to be an anomaly, but I felt more relaxed knowing it was a girl.

We received a few photos of the baby, checked out of the doctor's office and left. When we arrived back to the center, Jillian and Charlotte were waiting for us, each with an envelope in their hands.

"I can't take the suspense any longer. What are you having?" Charlotte asked, as we approached.

"Hold on, you first. Y'all have known longer than I have," I told them.

"Why don't we say what we are having at the same time?" Jillian suggested.

"That's stupid. I'll go first. It's a girl!" Charlotte said.

"Me too," both Jillian and I said, simultaneously.

The three of us screamed, as Jasper stepped away to make a phone call. We hugged, but I kept my eye on Jasper between Charlotte and Jillians shoulders. His secret phone calls had increased since the murder. As my belly grew and the baby became more active, he had become more protective over me.

"What's that about?" Charlotte asked, pointing toward Jasper, who was standing just out of ear shot.

"I don't know. Maybe he is planning a secret baby shower for me?" I suggested.

"He seems to have been doing that a lot. Mark said Jasper has been pulling away and isn't as friendly as he was before," Jillian told me.

"I have noticed some differences in him since we got married, but it's more that he has been keeping a closer eye on me. He's just being protective because he loves me," I told them, almost as though I was trying to convince myself more than I actually believed it.

"It's more than that. It's the way he is looking at us right now. He looks like he is conspiring against us. It's almost as if he is trying to figure out a way to get Jillian and me away from you," Charlotte said.

"I don't think that's what he's doing," I said, more of questioning myself at that point.

"Just make sure that he doesn't try to keep you away from us," Jillian said, embracing me.

"That will never happen," I told her. "You have always been and will always be, my family. I would always choose the two of you and my children over anyone else."

Charlotte and Jillian walked into the dining area, as I headed toward Jasper. He quickly hung up his phone and smiled at me.

"So all three of you got pregnant around the same time and all three of you are having girls within weeks of each other. Isn't that nice?" Jasper told me.

"It is nice. It's so weird how different each one of our pregnancies have been, but all the babies are the same gender," I said.

"Well, all women are different, so each one of your pregnancies will be different. Let's go to our room and rest up. You look tired," Jasper said, leading me toward the stairs.

I wasn't really tired, but I followed him anyway. Once we had entered the room, I lay down on the bed and Jasper cuddled in behind me. I felt as though maybe I was being irrational. He placed his hand gently over my belly. Jasper loved me and he loved our little girl. I didn't think he was trying to take away any of my family, but because they were concerned enough to mention it, I was going to keep an eye on him.

Twenty Three

As I was entering my third trimester, Jasper and I were beginning a list of names for our daughter. He had his list and I had mine. Every couple of days we would share our lists with each other and veto which names we didn't like.

We were expecting Jillian to deliver her baby any day and I was keeping my phone close by just in case Mark called to let us know he had taken her to the hospital. She had been spending the past two weeks at home. Her husband was watching her like a hawk and any slight pain she had, he would immediately fall to her side to be sure she was okay.

Charlotte was on bed rest as her doctor felt as though she was at high risk. At seven months she was already eight centimeters dilated and the doctor was worried she could go into labor early and at the time, her baby was breech. The doctor was hoping the baby would turn on her own, but wanted Charlotte to take it easy to ensure the baby had time to turn head down.

Since I was still a few weeks out from delivery, I was scrolling mommy groups on social media for second hand items that I knew were only used for a few months before an infant would grow out of using the item. I wanted a swing, bassinet and bouncy seat, along with a few blankets maybe and possibly newborn onesies.

I was contacted by a woman named Diane Smith who had a swing and bouncy chair that she was willing to sell for ten dollars each. I was intrigued by her offer, so I messaged her back.

'Hello Diane. Thank you so much for your offer. I was just wondering, how old are the items and how long were they used?' I messaged.

'I have three children. The oldest is now ten and my youngest is two. I bought the items when I was pregnant with my oldest, but she didn't like either, so with her, they were only used a couple of times. With both my boys, it was the only way to keep them quiet and they used them for six months each. Thank you for your reply,' she answered.

'Is there any way we could negotiate the price down to fifteen for both?'

'That's fine. Let me get you my address and phone number in case you get lost. See you soon.'

When I found out she lived across town, I was grateful she had contacted me. I had received two other messages from people who lived in different states. They weren't willing to ship the items to me and I was beginning to lose hope.

We had planned to meet up by the end of the week and I felt as though I was another step closer to being prepared for my little girl. I added the meeting to my calendar, then left my office and walked out to the reception area. As I sat behind the desk, I watched the parking lot through the windows of the front doors.

I looked around, trying to figure out where Jasper went. Last I knew, he was loitering around the reception area because he didn't want me to be alone. I shrugged, thinking that he may have gone upstairs for some reason.

As I was zoning out, staring out the window, I saw a white paneled van pull up to the front doors. The center was quiet as Charlotte and Jillian were at home and Gabrielle was assisting Mark with setting up the nursery before Jillian went into labor.

There was a young teenage boy who exited the passenger side of the van. He opened the back sliding door as he waited for the driver to walk around the back of the van.

The driver was an older woman who appeared to be in her early to mid-forties. She stopped in front of the open side door to the van and talked to the boy. After a few moments, they both entered the front doors to the center and approached the reception desk where I sat.

"Hello, Mackenzie," the woman said, as they stopped in front of the desk.

"Hello, how can I help you?" I responded cordially, as I stood up.

"You have been damaged and emotionally broken. You must repent, or you will spend the rest of your life running from danger," the woman said.

"Excuse me?" I said, confused.

"You must repent," the boy said, making direct eye contact with me.

"You must give up your daughter for adoption to ensure she is raised by someone who is not emotionally unstable," the woman continued.

"I'm sorry, who are you and how do you know my baby is a girl?" I wanted to know.

"You must repent," the boy repeated.

"You have a limited time to make the right decision. Come with us and give up your baby once she is born, or stay here and face the consequences. The choice is yours," the woman told me.

"I'm done with your riddles," I said, before picking up the phone on the desk and calling Agent Leigh.

"You must repent," the boy's voice boomed throughout the center and banging his fist down on the desk, as Leigh answered my call.

"Can you send the police here to the center? I have an emergency and I don't know where Jasper is," I told her.

"What's going on?" Leigh asked.

"I have a couple of people standing in front of me, threatening me and my baby," I explained.

"Where are you in the center?" Leigh wanted to know.

"I'm at the reception desk. They are standing in front of me on the other side of the reception desk," I informed her.

"Don't step out from behind the desk. You could be safer in the cube," she told me.

"Is there a problem out here?" Mary Hinson said, appearing at the stair landing.

"This matter does not concern you," the strange woman told Mary.

"You must repent," the boy was now shouting.

"It concerns me when your hostile behavior scares my children," Mary warned, as she began stepping down the few final steps.

"It's okay Mary. I'm on the phone with Agent Leigh. She's sending the police. Go upstairs and take care of your children," I told her, without looking away from the intruders that stood in front of me.

"They are with Lavender. They should be fine. I think I'll just wait here with you, for law enforcement to arrive," Mary said, as she stepped up behind me.

"The police should be there. I'm still about five minutes out. Have they come through the door yet?" Leigh asked.

"I can see a couple of uniformed officers looking at the van outside right now," I said, as the woman and the boy continued to glare at me.

"You must repent," the boy shouted again.

"Could you please stop shouting?" I politely asked the boy.

"Try not to engage with them," Leigh told me.

"YOU MUST REPENT!" the boy shouted and slammed his fist down on the desk so hard, all the items rattled on the desk.

"Okay, I just pulled into the parking lot. I'll be in, in just a moment," Leigh said, before hanging up the phone.

"Repent, repent, repent, repent," both visitors began chanting as soon as I put the phone down.

Twenty Four

The chanting gained the attention of the uniformed officers outside and most of the guests at the center. The guests began to gather along the stairs and on the landing. After the police cleared the van, they entered through the front doors, with Agent Leigh close behind.

"Let me see your hands," one officer yelled, as they both placed their hands on their side arms.

The two stopped chanting and slowly turned around. The officers and Leigh drew their guns and pointed them at the strangers. Mary and I stepped out from behind the reception desk and joined the other guests near the stairs.

"Put your hands up," Leigh insisted.

The strangers begrudgingly complied, by raising their hands in line with their shoulders. They slowly stepped toward the officers. Once they were within arms reach, the officers holstered their weapons and grabbed the intruders. The two were then handcuffed and led outside to their van.

"Are you alright?" Leigh asked, holstering her gun and quickly walking toward me.

"I think so," I said, tears welling up in my eyes.

"Do you know them?" Mary asked.

"I have no idea who they are. They told me to repent and put my baby up for adoption because I'm damaged," I said, crying uncontrollably.

"Okay everyone, head back to your rooms. The situation has been handled," Agent Leigh announced, as Mary consoled me.

The guests dispersed, some went back upstairs, while others went into the common areas to gossip. Mary and Leigh lead me into my office.

"Where is Jasper?" Leigh asked, after I had sat down behind my desk and her and Mary sat across from me in the guest chairs.

"I don't know. He was suppose to be here in the reception area," I informed her, wiping my face and nose with a tissue.

"Have you tried calling him?" Mary asked.

"You might want to call him and let him know what has transpired and find out where he went," Leigh said, as she stood up, frustrated.

"I left my cell phone on the reception desk," I said, as I patted my pockets.

"Don't worry, I'll get it," Mary said, standing and walking out to the reception area.

I watched out my office window as one of the uniformed officers came back inside and encouraged Leigh to step out of the office. The two of them walked out to the reception area, as Mary re-entered my office.

"What!" Leigh exclaimed, after she spoke with the officer for a couple of minutes.

The uniformed officer nodded, as Leigh rubbed her face. I held off calling Jasper, waiting to hear what the officer told her. Leigh turned to look at me through the window, as the officer headed back out of the center. Leigh lowered her head and returned to my office.

"Mary, can you please excuse us for a moment. I need to speak to Mackenzie privately," Leigh requested.

"Absolutely. Mackenzie, I will be in my room with my children if you need me," Mary told me, before leaving the office.

"What happened?" I asked, when Leigh closed the door and sat down.

"Well, you know the woman," Leigh told me, as she leaned back in the chair.

"Who is she? Oh god, don't tell me I have another biological family member that has decided to come back into my life."

"No, it's nothing like that. She's Angela."

"What the fuck? Cult member, foster sister, Angela?" I wondered.

"The one and only. You didn't recognize her at all?" Leigh asked.

"Of course not. It's been like thirty years since I've seen her."

"Well, I can tell you, unfortunately, we can't charge them with anything."

"Why not?"

"They walked into a public building, so they weren't trespassing. They didn't touch you in any way, so it's not assault. I'm sorry, but we can't charge them with a crime, but we can question them as to why they came in here and threatened you. The law is vague as to what we can do in this situation."

"Technically, both me and my baby were being threatened. Can't they be arrested for making threats?"

"If threatening someone was an arrest-able offense, our jails would be full of people who made empty threats out of anger," Leigh commented.

"So in other words, I have to wait for them to actually act on their threats. What if they try to kidnap my daughter?" I said, wrapping my arms around my belly.

"Well, you still have a little while before she is outside of your body, so we can hope they lose interest before that time comes."

"I have already been cut open when I was pregnant the first time. There are a few cases of women having their babies cut out of their bellies. I fear that this could happen to me again."

"It does happen, but it's rare. They seem to be more interested in being sure that you have a healthy baby."

"Right, because they seem interested in my baby's well being. It seems as though their persistence has ramped up since I last spoke to Amber."

"Have you heard from her recently? I'm a little concerned. She sounded terrified the last time I talked to her," Leigh inquired.

"I haven't heard from her for months. I figured she finally got the hint. I told her to stop calling me," I told Leigh.

"I'll contact the local police department where she lives to do a welfare check on her."

"I don't know why you should care. You're the one who told her to leave town and never talk to me again."

"Well, that doesn't mean I didn't keep an eye on her. I felt bad that all in one day, she lost her entire family and found out her father was a psychopath. I wanted to make sure she was able to get her life together and be self sustainable."

"I get it. So, who was the boy with Angela?"

"Her sixteen year old son, Charlie. He was born in the cult and only knows what he grew up being told," Leigh explained.

"I don't blame him. I blame the family he was born into. I thought Angela was stronger than that. How could she allow herself to be brainwashed?" I wanted to know.

"The human mind is a complex organ. If you go into survival mode, you could be convinced of anything. Plus, I feel as though she is suffering from a case of Stockholm Syndrome," Leigh explained.

"Regardless of that, how did they know I am having a girl?" I asked.

"It could have just been a guess. They had a fifty-fifty chance of guessing the gender. Potentially they didn't really know."

"Angela was pretty confident when she said I needed to give my daughter up for adoption."

"Well, let's put the situation behind us. You need to call Jasper and find out where he went."

I nodded, shrugged my shoulders and called Jasper. The first time I called, he sent me to voicemail. I called him a second time immediately.

"Are you okay?" Jasper asked, when he finally answered.

"Where are you? You were suppose to be here at the center making sure there isn't any danger," I scolded.

"Nothing was going on, so I thought I would go out to get you something to eat. I'll be back soon. What happened?" Jasper explained.

"Two people walked into the center and threatened me and our daughter. You weren't here and they disrupted the guests," I told him, crying.

"Did they hurt you?" he asked.

"I was a little shaken up at first, but Mary backed me up and once Leigh and the police showed up, I was okay. Leigh is here with me now. She just wanted me to find out where you were and inform you about the situation," I told him.

"I'm on my way home now," Jasper said.

"Leigh is going to assign a protective detail for me, so this doesn't happen again and when I go out to pick up a few things for the baby, I will have an armed guard."

"Are you sure that's necessary? I promise I will never leave you again without telling you first."

"That's not the problem. The problem was the fact that you left me here without anyone. You knew there was a potential for danger."

"I'm sorry. I'm on my way home right now. Don't go anywhere. I want you to stay in the safety of the center," Jasper said.

"I have a few things I need to do. Gabrielle is coming by to watch reception so I can go out and pick up a couple of things for our baby. I'm taking the protective detail with me and I'll be back later," I told him.

"You make sure that officer stays with you."

"I will, I promise."

"Were did he go?" Leigh asked, as I hung up the phone.

"He said that since nothing was going on, he left to go get me something to eat," I told her.

"Have you eaten breakfast?" Leigh wanted to know.

"Yes, but I didn't want to eat lunch two hours afterward. I feel like it was just an excuse," I said, just as Gabrielle knocked on my office door.

I waved her in and received a message notification. I looked down at my phone to see that Diane Smith had messaged me. I opened the message and read that she wanted to meet me later that afternoon.

I responded, telling her I would be happy to, then gave a run down of the situation to Gabrielle.

"I don't think Matthew would allow anything to happen to your little girl. He says they are meant to be best friends just like you were friends with his mother," Gabrielle said, giggling.

"That would be great. He would definitely protect her," I told Gabrielle.

"Your protective detail is here, Mackenzie. Come on, let's go meet him," Leigh told me, leading me out of the office.

Twenty Five

Leigh introduced me to the plain clothes officer that was waiting for me in the reception area. He was armed and he was to go everywhere I go.

"Mackenzie, this is Bert. He's going to be your shadow for as long as you need him," Leigh introduced.

"Well, hello Bert. I hope you don't mind to go shopping for some baby stuff," I said, extending my hand.

"No ma'am, I don't mind," Bert said, shaking my hand.

"Good, let's go," I told him, heading toward the front door.

Bert was a good looking man and I didn't mind having him chaperone me around. I gave him the address to Diane Smith's house and we climbed into his car. He didn't say much the whole ride, but it was peaceful. I was a little in awe of him, so I wasn't sure what to say.

As he pulled up to the home, I had an uneasy feeling. My little girl was doing summersaults in my belly. It was as if she could sense my tension.

"You're going to be staying with me the whole time, right?" I asked Bert.

"I will be right next to you the whole time. If you feel uncomfortable, we can leave," he told me.

"I think I'm just a little jittery from what happened back at the center."

"Just remember, I'm here to keep you safe. I won't let anything happen to you."

I nodded, as we both exited the vehicle and headed up to the front door. As I hesitated, Bert kept watch on the street. Just as I lifted my arm to knock, the door opened and a woman, only slightly older than me, stood on the other side.

"Are you Diane Smith?" I asked.

"Yes ma'am. You must be Mackenzie Tully. Come on in and I'll show you what I have," the woman said.

Bert turned and followed me into the stranger's home. Diane walked across the living room and showed me an infant swing and bouncy chair.

"Who is this?" Diane asked, referring to Bert.

"He's with me," I told her, as I walked over and bent down to check out the merchandise.

"Is it necessary for him to be in my house?" Diane asked.

"I'm not going anywhere, so just show the lady the items, or we're leaving," Bert told her.

"How old are the items?" I asked, trying to finish the transaction.

Before I could stand back up, I heard the sound of glass shattering and someone wrapped a belt around my neck and pulled me down, onto my back. I was dragged down a hallway and into the kitchen.

I saw Bert was laying on the floor behind the sofa, blood was seeping from a cut on his scalp. I struggled as best I could, grasping at my neck, trying to loosen the noose.

My baby girl was kicking me as hard as she could for as long as she could. As I struggled to get free, her movements became slower and not as strong. My baby girl was struggling and I was not going to let anyone take her from me.

Twenty Six

As I gasped for air, I thought that I was hallucinating. There were three people standing over me; I saw Angela, her son Charlie and the woman who claimed her name was Diane. Just behind them, I could have sworn I saw Jasper.

"You should have listened to me," Angela said, pulling a large chopping knife out of a butcher block on the counter.

"Ease up around her neck, Charlie. I want the baby unharmed," the figure of what looked like Jasper said.

"Angela, please. All I want to do is protect my baby. I can't protect her if I don't know where she is," I said, as Charlie loosened the belt around my neck.

"Gwen, Charlie, hold her down," Angela told them.

"Wait, Gwen?" I said, stupefied.

The one who told me her name was Diane, turned out to actually be Gwen. She positioned herself down by my legs and Charlie pinned down my arms.

"Remove her left leg, Gwen," Jasper told her.

I was beginning to realize that Jasper was not a figment of my imagination, but he was actually there and he was helping them. Gwen yanked my prosthetic loose and tossed it to the side.

"Jasper, help me," I cried out. "Angela, Gwen, why are you doing this to me?"

"Oh Mackenzie. Are you surprised that Gwen and I are still together? When you screwed up the foster home we were in, I thought Gwen and I were going to have a shitty life. We were actually adopted by a wonderful couple who showed us what family was really suppose to be like. When we turned eighteen, we had been arranged to marry an elder at our church. Luckily, it was the same guy, so we are sister wives," Angela told me.

"Jasper, how do you fit into all of this?" I wanted to know.

"Get on with it. I want to get my little girl and get out of here," Jasper ordered.

"Jasper, are you a part of their cult?" I asked him, even though he wasn't responding to me.

"It's not a cult!" Angela yelled. "Just because we had an arranged marriage within a church compound, does not mean we are in a cult."

"Why are you doing this to me?" I wondered.

"We only need your baby. We want to make sure she is taken care of properly," Angela informed.

"I can take care of her properly. You just have to let me go," I told her.

"No, you can't. Danger always finds you. We are going to take the baby with us so she can be raised in an environment with several mothers to keep her safe from danger," Gwen said, still holding down my right leg and left stump.

"Right now you are the one putting me in danger," I told Gwen, lifting my head up to look at her.

As I looked passed Gwen, I saw Jasper looking down at Angela, as if he was trying not to make eye contact with me. Bert began to stir on the floor. I was so glad he was still alive.

"Fuck this. Shut up. I'm taking your baby and there is nothing you can do about it," Angela said, before placing the blade of the knife along my lower abdomen.

As she sliced into my skin, I screamed as loud as I could muster in order to gain the attention of the officer as he slowly sat up. Just as I felt the blood begin to pool around me and soak my pants, Bert was on his feet and he was pulling his gun out of its holster.

"Quit screaming. I have to cut deeper to get the baby out," Angela scolded.

Since the front door had been left open, Bert got their attention, by slamming the door closed. Angela stood up and pointed the bloody knife toward the front door.

"Put down your weapon," the officer said, with authority, as he took two steps toward the kitchen pointing his gun straight out in front of him.

"This is none of your business," Angela told him.

"Put down the knife," the officer repeated.

"Fuck you," Angela spouted.

Bert was leaning his hip against the back of the sofa, aiming his gun toward Angela and Jasper, trying to steady himself. Gwen let go of my leg and stump, backing away from me and stepped over next to Jasper. Charlie let go of my arms and joined Gwen and Jasper.

Without taking his eyes off of Angela, Bert pulled out his cell phone and called his dispatch. When he requested an ambulance, Angela crouched down again between my legs. She pressed the blade of the knife to my stomach and sliced across the initial cut, only deeper the second time. The screeching sound that emanated from my voice was a sound I had never made before that moment.

"Stop right there. Put down the knife," Bert ordered Angela.

She quickly stood and lunged at him, knife in hand and slashed his forearm. Out of reflex, Bert pulled the trigger on his gun and shot her through her shoulder. Angela dropped the knife and Charlie pulled away from Jasper in order to grab a towel off the counter. He rushed over and pressed it against his mother's wound. He assisted Angela over to where Jasper and Gwen were standing.

I tried to pull myself up on my elbows, but the gash in my abdomen burned and I yelled out in pain. I lay flat on my back, with my hands on my belly just above the make shift cesarian. My little girl was no longer moving and I immediately began to fear the worst.

"The ambulance is on its way, Mackenzie. Just hold on a little longer," Bert encouraged me.

Jasper, Angela, Charlie and Gwen were huddled against the wall between the kitchen and living room. Jasper hadn't looked at me, or even acknowledged my presence throughout the entire attack.

I could feel blood seeping through my clothes and I focused on my breathing, along with staying awake, as I heard the approaching sirens. The front door swung open, tears rolling down my temples as I blinked quickly and moved my hands down to the sides of my pregnant belly.

"Get those four over there," Bert ordered the officers who rushed in.

"Hey, watch my shoulder. I've been shot," Angela complained.

Six uniformed officers handcuffed my attackers and led them outside. Angela was the only voice I heard as they were taken away. Bert replaced his gun in his side holster and rushed into the kitchen.

"Stay with me, Mackenzie," Bert told me, as he sat down on the floor next to me and held my hand.

"Is my baby going to be okay?" I asked Burt.

"She's going to be okay. You're going to be okay. Just breathe and focus on me. The ambulance just arrived. They're coming in now," Bert reassured me.

Two EMT's rushed into the house with a gurney. They shooed Bert away from me, so they could each get next to me. They did what they could to contain the bleeding before I was gently transferred to a back board, then lifted onto the gurney.

"What's your name?" one EMT asked.

"Mackenzie. Mackenzie Tully," I said, between painful breaths.

"Well Mackenzie, I'm Terry and this is Nora. We are going to help you. How far along are you?" the EMT wondered.

"Thirty weeks," I told him.

"From what I can see here, she barely broke the skin and didn't nick the amniotic sac. We are going to take you to the hospital to make sure the baby is okay," Nora told me.

"Please, save my baby," I told them.

"I just contacted Agent Leigh. She's going to meet us at the hospital. I will be in my car right behind the ambulance," my protective detail told me, as Terry and Nora wheeled me out.

"No, please. Don't leave me alone," I pleaded with him.

"Mackenzie, listen to me," Nora said, stroking my hair. "Officer Bert needs medical attention to the laceration on his head and the wound on his arm. As soon as he is looked at and cleared, he will be able to meet you at the hospital. Terry and I will be with you in the back of the ambulance and I will make sure someone is with you before I leave you at the hospital. Are you okay with that?"

I nodded as the gurney I was on was slid into the back of the ambulance. Bert kept an eye on me until the back doors to the ambulance were closed and he could no longer see me.

Twenty Seven

On the way to the hospital, I felt as though I was having an out of body experience. I was awake and aware of what was happening, but I was unable to respond to the medical technicians. They cleaned and bandaged my wound as best as they could with what they had inside the ambulance.

As I arrived at the hospital, the staff was prepared to hook me up to the fetal monitor machines. They placed straps over my large pregnant belly to monitor not only the baby's heart rate, but also to monitor any contractions I may have.

Faith arrived a few minutes after the nurse checked all the monitors and was leaving the room. She rushed passed the nurse and wrapped her arms around me.

"Oh my god. Are you okay?" she asked, as she pulled away and placed her hands on my belly.

"I'm more worried about my little girl," I told her, tears streaming down my face.

"Mackenzie Tully, which room is she in?" I heard Bert's voice, from out in the hallway at the nurses station.

"Bert, right here," Leigh told him, as she poked her head out into the hallway.

"Oh, thank goodness. Mackenzie, how are you doing? How's the baby?" Bert inquired, as he walked passed Leigh and straight to my bedside.

"She has a heartbeat, so it's still promising. The doctor says the incision went through to the muscle, but didn't puncture my uterus. If you hadn't stopped Angela when you did, she would have gone in a third time and could have punctured my uterus and the amniotic sac. I have been stitched up and we are hoping it will heal within the next two to four weeks, so I can have the natural birth I want," I informed him.

"Well, I got five stitches in my head and I'm all patched up. I will not leave your side until we are sure you are out of danger," Bert told me, grabbing my hand.

"Thank you, Bert. I appreciate your dedication," I told him, squeezing his hand.

"So Angela and Charlie lured you into their house, using Gwen?" Leigh asked.

"It's because they knew I wouldn't recognize Gwen. I had no idea who Angela was when she approached me in the center. It's almost as if that was a test as to whether or not I would know who they were after all these years. They knew I was having a girl because of Jasper," I explained, crying uncontrollably.

"Jasper? Jasper was involved in this?" Leigh asked, dumbfounded.

"I think he's the one who knocked me out," Bert informed.

"He was ordering Angela as to what he wanted her to do. When you investigated Angela and Gwen, did you find anything that would have connected them to Jasper?" I questioned Leigh.

"There wasn't anything to indicate they knew each other in any way. I can check to see if Jasper's adoptive parents were associated with the same religious group," Leigh suggested.

"You may have to do that anyway. When this goes to court, they might want to know if there is a connection. Mackenzie, how did you and Jasper meet?" Bert said.

"A couple of years ago we met at a diner. We had gone on a few dates, then he revealed that he was from my past. I grew up bouncing around foster homes and group homes. There was one group home where I thought I had found my soul mate. I knew him as Jojo. Jasper told me he was Jojo. I loved him when I was a kid and all those feelings came back when Jasper told me he was Jojo," I explained, grieving the loss of my love.

"Agent Leigh, do you know who Jasper's adoptive parents are?" Bert asked.

"I will be looking into it," Leigh said.

"Detective Rage gave me a run down back when we first started dating," I informed, wiping my face.

"Are you sure that information was true? It could have been possible that Brett Carter/Detective Rage could have brought Angela and Jasper in to ensure that you would eventually meet your demise," Leigh informed.

"This is a lot. Do I need to bring Rebecca in on this to find out who Brett Carter really was? I don't know how much more I can take," I said, taking a deep breath.

"I don't know if Rebecca needs to be brought in on this situation. I'm going to do a plethora of research and see if there is any connection between them. I don't want to include Rebecca, just in case she is somehow involved," Leigh admitted, before stepping out of the room.

"You have really gone through some shit in your life, haven't you," Bert said.

"I just want it to stop. Am I destined to live a life where I can't trust anyone and I have to constantly look over my shoulder?" I inquired.

"I can assure you, you can trust me. As long as I'm around, nothing will happen to you, or your daughter," Bert assured me.

Twenty Eight

Bert stayed with me in the hospital, as I was healing from the womb raider botch job. My little girl regained her strength after a few days. The doctor was worried that if she got any bigger, it could potentially stretch my belly and reopen the wound. I was scheduled to be induced at thirty two weeks.

"I need to call Jillian and Charlotte. They need to know that my little girl is coming early," I told Bert.

"Tom and Mark said they would bring the girls by to see you. They should be here soon," Bert informed me.

"You already called? Thank you Bert," I said.

After about an hour Mark wheeled a very pregnant Jillian into the room, with Charlotte and Tom close behind. Bert and Tom assisted Charlotte into a chair.

"How far along are you now, Jillian?" I asked.

"Thirty nine weeks. I just want her out already," Jillian complained.

"I'm at thirty five weeks and I feel the same way," Charlotte said, placing her hand on her belly.

"In six days, I am being induced. The doctor is worried about my little girl stretching out my belly any more and possibly reopening the wound," I told them.

"So what the hell happened with Jasper?" Tom blurted.

"Tom, we talked about this on the way over. You weren't supposed to mention it," Charlotte scolded, backhanding her husband on his thigh, as he stood next to her.

"It's okay, I understand. Faith is looking into it and she will tell me what she finds, once I am home after the baby is born," I told them.

"Good, so that means we don't have to talk about this right now," Jillian said, hunching over and grabbing her belly. "I think I might be in labor."

Mark grabbed the wheel chair and wheeled Jillian out to the nurses station as she breathed through her contractions. Charlotte and Tom stayed in the room with me and Bert stood in the doorway, keeping watch.

"How crazy would it be if our girls were all born in the same week?" Charlotte said, rubbing her belly.

"Do they have a name picked out?" I wondered.

"I don't know. Jillian said they wanted it to be a surprise," Charlotte told me.

"What about you? Do you have a name picked out?" I asked.

"We do, but I think we are going to keep it a surprise as well," Tom said.

"Oh you do, do you?" Charlotte said, laughing. "It's not a secret, or anything."

"Jasper and I had come up with a name for our little girl, but I don't want to use it anymore. I don't want to give him the satisfaction of having any sort of connection to my baby. She's *my* baby," I cried.

"Okay Mackenzie, do you want to get some sleep?" Bert asked, as he stepped back into the room.

"No, I'm fine. I'm sorry. I guess it's all hitting me right now. I'm going to be a single mother now. All my kids back at the center will no longer have a male role model to look up to. How are they doing? Is Kensington doing okay without me there? Is Lavender able to handle any issues they might be dealing with? Do they need me to come home, because I could probably get the doctor to allow me to rest at home if the kids need me," I inquired.

"Gabrielle is frustrating Lavender. She said if you don't come back soon, she's going to leave with her sisters," Charlotte informed me.

"Bert, while Charlotte and Tom are here, will you please run over to the center and get Lavender. Maybe if you bring her here with me, I can talk to her and reassure her that she is wanted. I don't want her to leave. I can't lose any of my children now. Also, please check on Kensington. He seems to have a hard time if I am gone for too long," I requested.

"I will call Agent Leigh and have Lavender brought here. I won't leave you unprotected. Don't worry

Mackenzie, I will help you get your life back together," Bert told me, before stepping out of the room.

"So, what's the deal with Bert?" Tom asked.

"Nothing is the deal with Bert. He is the protective detail that Faith has given me. He's here to make sure I don't get hurt again," I told them.

"I think he likes you," Tom said, raising his eye brows at me.

"I just want to focus on my children. That's it," I told him, pursing my lips.

"She's here! Pricilla Renee has been born. Six pounds, nine ounces, nineteen and a half inches long. Both baby and momma are doing great and will be able to go home in a couple of days," Mark announced, as he ran into the room.

"That's great! Holy shit that was fast! When can we see her?" Charlotte asked.

"I think Jillian was in labor last night, even though she wouldn't admit it. If her labor started last night, that would mean that she had been in labor for over twelve hours. By the time we were able to get into the labor and delivery room, she was already ten centimeters dilated and the nurse immediately moved into delivery mode. Jillian has decided that she wants to spend some alone time with the baby first. She said she will bring the baby here before we leave," Mark informed, before leaving the room.

"I'm so glad that she has decided to spend some alone time with her little girl before others want to hold the baby. It gives her the initial bonding quiet time. Birth can be very chaotic and if Jillian is relaxed for the first few hours of her little girl's life, it could set the mood for her whole life. It could reduce anxiety and awkward social interactions," I commended Jillian's decision.

"You don't think she is being selfish by withholding us from seeing the baby?" Charlotte complained.

"Not at all. Think about it, you have spent nine months relaxing and growing without a care in the world, to all of a sudden having to breathe on your own. And to top it off, it's cold and you're probably hungry and there are bright lights in your face. Wouldn't you prefer a calm, relaxing birthday?" I asked.

"Okay, I get your point. Maybe I will do the same thing," Charlotte said.

"I hope you do. We can all meet up at the center and show off our babies. Why would you want a bunch of people poking at your brand new baby hours after she was expelled from your body?" I mentioned, feeling a Braxton Hicks contraction and breathing through it.

"Are you okay, Mackenzie?" Bert asked, as he poked his head in the door.

"I'm fine. She just shifted," I lied. "Is Faith on her way with Lavender?"

"They should be here shortly," Bert told me.

"Do you know if they were bringing Kensington with them?" I asked.

"I told Leigh to check on him and use her judgement on whether or not he needed to see you," Bert informed me.

"Thank you," I told him, holding my hand out to get him to come back into the room.

Bert stepped over to the opposite side of the bed from where Charlotte and Tom were and grabbed my hand. I was thankful that he was there and glad that I had made a new friend. Faith had to know that we would get along when she assigned him to be my protective detail.

A few moments later, Leigh walked into the room with Lavender. She stood at the foot of the bed. I could see the irritation on her face. I knew that she wasn't irritated with me, but I wanted to make sure she knew I would be coming home soon.

"Are you doing okay? How is everything going at the center? Are the kids okay?" I asked Lavender.

"Kensington is having a hard time without you, but Avalina and Zarabella are doing their best to help him relax," she told me.

"And how are you?" I asked.

"Gabrielle is getting on my damn nerves. I have had to tell her that I am an adult and she doesn't need to tell me what to do. If she continues to treat me like a child, I will be taking my sisters and leave the center. That bitch is not my mother, you are," Lavender told me, touching my foot.

"I don't appreciate the language, but I will let it slide because you said I am your mother," I said, with tears welling up.

"Of course you are," Lavender said, stepping around to the side of the bed and sat up near my feet. "You are the mother to all of us at the center. We love you."

"I promise you, I will always be there for you and all my children that reside at the center. Please don't leave. If I speak with the medical staff, how would you feel about staying with me until my baby is born?" I asked Lavender, knowing she never really got along with Gabrielle.

Twenty Nine

Three days after Pricilla was born, Jillian brought her into the room to see us. As Charlotte stood to get a good look at the new bundle, her water broke and she was rushed to a delivery room.

"She's so small," Lavender said, as she held the new baby.

"I'm pretty sure Mackenzie's baby will be smaller," Jillian informed Lavender.

"Is she okay?" Lavender asked, passing Pricilla back to Jillian.

"She's okay. The doctor is more concerned about me. She doesn't want the baby to grow too big and potentially rip open the wound on my stomach," I told her.

"Are they at least going to make sure that it is safe enough for her to survive outside of your body?" Lavender worried.

"Absolutely. I have an appointment tomorrow for one of those fancy ultrasounds," I informed her.

"Thank goodness for that," Lavender said, laying down on the bed next to me.

"Penelope Grace is here!" Tom announced, a couple of hours later. "Five pounds, four ounces, eighteen and a quarter inches long. She's a little small, but she is a few weeks early. Momma and baby are doing great."

"I'm so excited! Our little girls can have joint birthdays!" Jillian squealed.

"That will be something to discuss with Charlotte," I said, laughing.

"So, Jillian has Pricilla and Charlotte has Penelope, what name did you choose Mackenzie?" Lavender asked.

"I was waiting to see what names they had chosen, so I wouldn't pick the same name. The three of us must be so connected because I was trying to decide between Piper and Paisley," I revealed.

"All three of you are going to have children with names that start with the letter P," Lavender laughed.

"Do you have a suggestion?" I asked her.

"What was the name you chose with Jasper?" she inquired.

"I'm not using it. I don't want to use that name," I said, tears pooling in my eyes.

"I didn't say you had to use it. I just want to know," Lavender said.

"Forget it. I'll figure it out on my own," I said, rubbing my face.

"For what it's worth, I like the name Paisley," Bert said, from the doorway.

"Thank you Bert. See Lavender, that was helpful," I told her, as she rolled her eyes.

Three days later, at thirty two weeks, I was induced and my little girl made her appearance out into the world being delivered early, but healthy. Paisley May was born at four pounds, two ounces, fifteen and three quarter inches long. She had to spend her first week in the hospital.

Bert drove Lavender and I with Paisley, back to the center once we were released. When we walked in, everyone was waiting for us in the reception area to meet the new baby.

Leigh had done some digging and although Jasper was adopted, he was not the Jojo that I knew. Jasper had been adopted by the same couple as Angela and Gwen, but it was two years before they were. It just so happened to be a couple who were related to the couple who adopted Malachi.

When Brett Carter murdered the couple and kidnapped Malachi; Jasper, Angela and Gwen showed up at the house when Brett was talking to Malachi. He told them to go home and that if they stayed quiet and didn't tell anyone what happened, he would come back for them someday when they were needed.

He convinced Jasper to date me, because he knew it would upset Malachi enough to attack me. This part of his plan was not shared with Amber. She had no idea that Malachi had been taken from a cult compound and didn't know that he had spoken to anyone else.

When Brett had first spoken to Angela and Gwen, he didn't know that they had previously come into contact with me. When Gwen first brought it up, Brett was pleased with himself and insisted they be the two who ruin my life. Angela and Gwen were told to stand by until Jasper informed them that I was pregnant. They were supposed to eliminate me and steal my baby.

It was Brett Carter's last fuck you to me. He did everything he could to get rid of the one child that he believed wasn't his, because Rebecca got rid of his two other children, Malachi and Amber. Jasper somehow found out about Jojo and managed to deceive me into believing that he was my childhood crush.

All the times that Jasper had snuck away to make secret phone calls, he was contacting Angela and Gwen. When he led Dustin, Sara, Camden and Hallie away from our table when we were on our honeymoon, he basically told them they were no longer needed. They were only there to make an appearance, so they could be used later on to bring Amber back into my life.

Amber was being used as a pawn in their sick game they were playing with me. Jasper used the opportunity of Jenny being alone in her room, to murder her and attempted to send me a sinister message. When he removed her uterus, it was his way of telling me that my baby would be stolen.

Leigh insisted that I be on high alert to anyone that I allow into my life from that point on. Considering that Jasper, Angela and Gwen come from a large cult family, they could at any point pass the gauntlet on to someone else. Luckily, Leigh decided to do a full background check on Bert before allowing him to continue to be my protective detail. She met his family and was relieved to find out that he was *not* adopted.

"Bert is going to be your full time armed guard. You and Paisley are not to be unguarded for any reason," Leigh told me.

"Seeing as I will absolutely not ever let my daughter out of my sight, how long are we going to be under watch?" I asked her.

"At this point, just until Jasper, Angela, Charlie and Gwen are tried and convicted. Once that happens and we can confirm your safety, you will no longer require the guard. On top of Bert personally guarding you and Paisley, you will also have a police officer at every door of the center," Leigh informed me.

"Thank you, Faith. I appreciate everything you have ever done for me, my entire life. You have been more of a mother to me than any other woman I have ever known. I would love it, if you would come visit us on a regular basis and be my little girl's gram," I requested.

"Mackenzie, I will always think of you like family. I guess now would be a good time to tell you. I will be retiring once these four scum bags are sentenced.

Would it be okay if I rent a room here after I retire, just so I can be closer to family?" Leigh asked.

"I would love for you to live here," I told her, crying as I hugged her.

That was it. Was I finally going to be able to live a normal life? Was this the end? How long would I feel safe before danger found me? As for now, I'm going to spend as much time with my baby girl and my foster children, so they know how much I love them and that I will always be there for them.